MW00990563

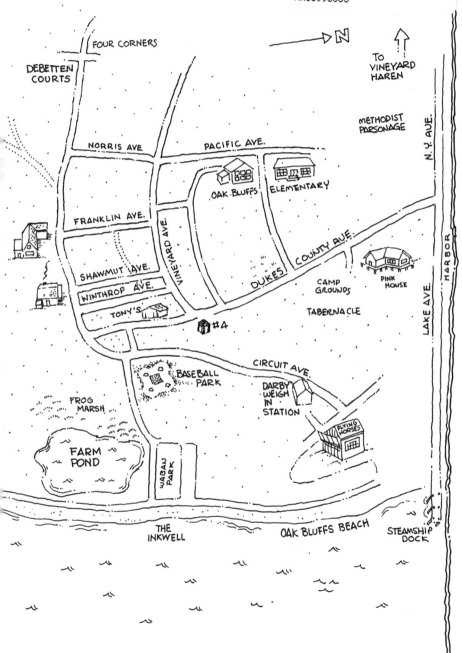

I had the Absolute Pleasure of meeting Susan Klein at a Dinner Party - 9-1-12 At the home of Virginia McClure

THROUGH A RUBY WINDOW

A Martha's Vineyard Childhood

Susan told a hilarious - talented story of her mom - that evening will always bring a smile to my heart

mom

9-10-12 I WAS SO PLEASED THAT Susan CAME To "Seasons" LAST evening to hear DAVID - we made plans

To meet Again —
hopefully in Deerfield, Fl.
at the end of March
2013 —

THROUGH A RUBY WINDOW

A Martha's Vineyard Childhood

by Susan Klein

AUGUST HOUSE PUBLISHERS, INC.
LITTLE ROCK

Published 1995 by August House, Inc.,
P.O. Box 3223, Little Rock, Arkansas, 72203,
501-372-5450.

Printed in the United States of America

10 9 8 7 6 5 4 3 2 1 HB

LIBRARY OF CONGRESS CATALOGUING-IN-PUBLICATION DATA
Klein, Susan, 1951-
Through a ruby window: a Martha's Vineyard
childhood / by Susan Klein.
p.   cm.
ISBN 0-87483-416-3 (HB) : $19.95
1. Martha's Vineyard (Mass.)—Social life and customs.
2. Klein, Susan, 1951- —childhood and youth.
3. Martha's Vineyard (Mass.)—Biography. I. Title.
F72.M5K57   1995
974.4'94—dc20   95-5234

Executive editor: Liz Parkhurst
Project editor: Rufus Griscom
Design director: Ted Parkhurst
Cover art and design: Harvill Ross Studios Ltd.
Cover Photo: Keith Kennedy

AUGUST HOUSE, INC.   PUBLISHERS   LITTLE ROCK

For "Jettche"
Else Henrietta Weinz Klein,
that wildly joyous and raucously opinionated
German weib who spawned me

Contents

Acknowledgments

THANKS TO NELSON for his definitive answers to my fishing questions, to my sister Eleanor for her lifelong support from the stands, and to both of you for your child-rearing savvy. Thanks to David Amaral for the affirmation that our childhood antics were as wild and varied as I remembered; and to Elsie Klein and Leisje Waldeyer for their hysterical oral history sessions.

Appreciation for their help with research goes to Jill Bouk of the Vineyard Museum, Robin Meader of the Flying Horses, and Rick Karney of the Martha's Vineyard Shellfish Group, as well as Stevie Sunfield, Mary Rapoza, and Bobbie-Ann Gibson.

Thanks to Keith Kennedy for the lovely cover photograph.

Thanks to the Sisters of Wisdom: Molly Kahn, Fanny McGrath, Jean Spencer, Ida Weinz, and Florence Wend for their legacy. Heartfelt thanks to Dr. Joyce Hancock, Dr. Annika Hurwitt, and Barbara Ivacek, for their clarity and foresight on this project, and to the Blue Mountain Group for the opportunity to develop professionally within a group of highly-respected peers.

Thanks to Milbre Burch, Jim May, and Jay O'Callahan for more than a dozen years of friendship and the encouragement to develop the Vineyard stories for performance, to the friends and audiences nationwide who affirmed the universality of the performance pieces, and finally to Ted and Liz Parkhurst of August House for their vision of the material in written form and for assigning this manuscript to Rufus Griscom, an editor with a much-appreciated sense of humor.

Introduction

THOUGH THE FORMAL NAME of the main street of Oak Bluffs is Circuit Avenue, it is teasingly referred to as "Circus" Avenue when the tourists are in town. During the years when I was growing up, the summer season clearly began the Fourth of July, though we had a promise of things to come on Memorial Day Weekend.

In summer we spent our days at the beach expanding our social circles to include summer friends here for a week or two, or some for the whole season. We rode the Flying Horses, ate our weight in fried clams and French fries from the summer takeout at Giordano's, and lazed away the days before we were old enough for summer jobs. At night we caught fireflies only to let them go, watching their blinking paths cross the yard, not knowing how blessed we were.

The family night out still practiced here included a drive downtown. The older children were sent to make purchases at Darling's Popcorn Store, a wonderfully archaic emporium. When the large doors were slid back, huge glass display cases trimmed with burgundy leather skirts, emblazoned in yellow with the words "Popcorn" and "Salt Water Taffy," were wheeled to the edge of the wooden boardwalk to become the front half-wall and open-air streetside sales counter. The smell of fresh snow-white popping corn drifted out to the street from the spout of the copper container that was bigger than I was, and the mechanical taffy pull twisted its colorful confection in midair. Munching foot-long chocolate, strawberry and caramel popcorn bars and salt water taffy, families parked on Circuit Avenue and watched the tourists stroll by. A running commentary on the looks of the off-islanders with their cameras, contrasting plaids, and strange ways filled the cars. The odder the parade of passing strangers, the more successful the evening out was thought to be.

The summers were filled with building camps in the woods, playing with friends and the joy of eating outside, where everything tasted better spiced with salt air. After the long-awaited West Tisbury agricultural fair occurred toward the end of August, summer waned and the sky turned azure.

The first Monday of September the doors of summer slammed shut. Everything that had buzzed and teemed with visitors just days before was closed up tight, boards and shutters closing out the autumn sun. The Strand Movie marquis and the Island Theatre were ghostly. The gift shops were empty; their leftover island-shaped ashtrays and souvenir trinkets had been dusted one last time and packed away. The remainder of the postcards were stored, the metal racks left standing in the vacant storefronts, the skeletons of summer.

The restaurants downtown, all seasonal except for Gerry's Coffee Shop and Mary's Restaurant, closed up with the advent of the fall semester, college stealing away the waitresses and kitchen help. Gerry DeBettencourt, of course, ran the coffee shop herself, offering a standard '50s menu of hamburgers, Cokes and daily home-cooked specials. I loved swiveling on the chrome and red leather stools. The townspeople loved the immaculate way she kept the place and the rapid-fire razzing that she served up with every order of fries. With a sweet smile Mary Goode served the best blueberry coffeecake in this corner of the solar system over her horseshoe counter.

Only the stores of necessity stayed open year-round. Pacheco's (Reliable Self-Service Market) and Phillips's Hardware Store were named for the families who ran them. The mere pronouncing of their names gave us a feeling of duration and constancy.

The 5 & 10 stayed open as well as daRosa's Print Shop, run by Mr. daRosa, a handsome and deceptively stern-looking man. Like great galleons, the printing presses pounded rhythmically amid a sea of aged wooden cabinets stuffed with metal print. A wall-to-wall display of haphazard stationery and art supplies lured lovers of language and color.

The high benches and brass shoe podiums outside Mr. Frye's Cobbler Shop stood as if on guard before the weathered cedar shingles and dark green trim that outlined a warm yellow light within. It seemed like an inviting forest cabin nestled in the middle of town. Inside, Mr. Frye's welcome encompassed us as quickly as the comfortable smells of leather and polish.

The windows of the rest of the buildings were boarded up

and looked as desolate as an abandoned mining town in some old Western. At night, all the year-round stores were closed and the street free of cars except for the area near the annual fishing derby weigh-in station and the Ritz, the local bar where folks gathered for a cold one or more, and sometimes to share their Friday paychecks, buying highballs and beer for their buddies, not always in service to the family budget.

Things have changed a great deal since then, some for the better, some not. The beginning and end of summer are no longer so distinct, nor are the year-rounders and visitors.

There's much more coming and going, more of everything now that the Vineyard keeps up with the times more readily than it ever cared to before. The one thing that has not changed is the magic that is laced through the sand, luring people to return again and again. It prompted one summer friend to say to me, "You can't know the thrill that fills me and every other summer visitor as the island comes into view for the first time in a year from the deck of the ferry."

I just smiled and thought to myself that that thrill is much like that felt by each islander as the Vineyard comes into view after shopping on the mainland for a day.

Through a Ruby Window

WHEN MY MOTHER AND I go beachplumming, the day is always clear and fine. The clarity and color of the sky are rivaled only by that of the sea, which has an unsurpassed richness of golden green and blue at that time of year.

Beachplums are a wild coastal crop, larger than blueberries, smaller than cherries. We gather the tart plums on the Vineyard in late summer when they are red-purple with a blush of frosting. We would have driven by that patch a time or two during the previous months to see how the beachplums were faring. I cannot tell you where the beachplums are; that would be sacrilege. Folks here on the island guard their beachplum locations with the fervor of pirates holding treasure maps. If it's a good year, the bushes will be loaded with plums and a harsh winter predicted. But if the harvest is lean, one might have to scout around a bit to find other bushes in order to have enough berries to make a year's worth of beachplum jelly. Secret locations abound.

When we reach our spot, my mother, who among family is affectionately known by her childhood nickname Jettche (pronounced Yecha), is out of the car before it stops. She grabs

whatever pot or pan or refrigerator crisper drawer is closest
and begins her litany of appreciation and delight.

"Ach du lieber Gott im Himmel!* Look at these beachplums! I can taste that shelleè just lookin' at 'em. Ach! They're
so vonderful! I can hardly vait!" Sixty years in America have
not erased her charming German accent, nor diminished the
liveliness of her speech.

She'll pick those marble-sized plums two-fisted, yakking
the whole time in celebration of their existence, and she won't
notice another thing until it's time to change buckets.

I choose the same spot with regularity each year and
slowly drop the first plums into my enamel pot. I love the first
sound of the plums, sort of a "boing" with a built-in thud.
When I've listened to enough enamel bucket music, I pick like
crazy.

Because I stand in one place and pivot at the knee, I get
cramped up if it's a bountiful season. So I crawl under the
bushes if I can, providing they are not intertwined with poison
ivy. Sometimes I find larger than usual beachplums, a happy
find, making the bucket fill faster.

Beachplumming is a no-nonsense activity. It's not like
blueberrying where one hand feeds the bucket and the other
the face. The first raw beachplum in the mouth is usually the
last. I know of no one who has eaten two. Like an unripe per-
simmon, a full-blown beachplum is tart enough to steal all the
saliva from your mouth and make you feel like your head
could turn inside out. Consequently, the amount picked is

* Oh, dear God in heaven!

equal to the amount transported home.

When I was a child, I always came home sunburned from a day of beachplumming. After receiving a hefty full body mother-applied smear of Noxema, I helped her make jelly.

First, we emptied all the fruit into what in my Portuguese neighborhood was called "the big blue *panela*." The big dark blue and white speckled enamel pot was filled with just enough water to cover the plums. They soaked overnight, allowing leaves, twigs, and errant insects to float to the surface.

The next morning, I woke to the sounds of my mother skimming the debris off the top and singing the same curious song she sang every morning that I can remember.

"And vhen we're dancink and you're dancherously near me, I ask you ple-ease, take off your ski-is."

I never understood it; I still don't.

I came downstairs as she finished pouring fresh water over the beachplums and set them on the "fire," the gas stove. Bread, butter, and apple jelly waited for me with a cup of coffee. No beachplum jelly was left by that time of year.

As I ate my breakfast, she added jars to another pot of boiling water on the stove. I loved to watch this, because Jettche hauled out all the jars she had been saving since the previous autumn. There were tall thin jars, short round jars, and some, no matter what you put in them, still triggered associations with what they originally contained, their shapes so closely identified with their contents.

She boiled them and, with tongs, took them out one by one and set them in the dish drain to dry. Then, after what always seemed like too long, the beachplums finally boiled and split, a light froth covering the top of the pot.

The largest Pyrex bowl sat on the kitchen counter with a three-footed aluminum colander standing in it. She ripped a piece of old but newly-laundered sheeting about two and a half feet square. She dampened it with tap water, shook it out, and laid it across the bowl, pushing the center of the cloth into the bottom of the colander.

Most folks used cheesecloth. But we used sheeting because in our house there was a mother-made rule that we must use everything over and over again. We didn't call it recycling. We called it "using stuff over and over again." My mother used to say, "Susie, if you vant to get rich, you better schtrike those matches tvice!"

The house filled with the hot, almost bitter scent of simmering beachplums. But only when she poured that pot of fruit pulp into the sheeting which I held secure, the steam momentarily blinding her by fogging up her glasses, did that marvelous aroma rush out the kitchen window and mingle with the same smells billowing through the kitchen screens of every other house on Wing Road.

The colander filled as the last trickle of juice poured over the pulp. The pot was empty, the bowl full. I held the four white corners of the cloth, the pink stain spreading in a circle outward across the bottom of the sheeting. Jettche wrapped packing twine two or three times around the ends close to the pulp, but not too close, and tied it as tightly as she could. Then I held the deep ruby sphere of piping hot pulp by the fabric beyond the knot, and Jettche made a sturdy loop with the twine. She hung the loop from a special jelly-making hook secured under the kitchen cabinet shelves.

The sheeting bulged, a satisfied belly. The juices streamed vermilion between the woven threads, glistening hot through the colander and into the bowl below.

While my mother cleaned up, I watched the juice escape until the stream became a steady drip, finally waning to a slow, nerve-wracking rhythm. Overnight, the bowl underneath filled with a deep purple juice. The pink spread to the taut twine but no further, leaving the pointed ends of percale bright white.

When I came down for breakfast the next day I immediately headed for the pulp bag. It was just yearning to be massaged.

"Ach du lieber Gott im Himmel! Du verrückte!* Vhat do you vant to do, ruin my shelleè?"

She unhooked the bag and handed it to me so I could squeeze it in the backyard, where the viscous pulp would not cloud her pristine fruit juice and prevent the jelly from setting clear. I eventually tired of kneading the gushy ball and loosened the twine just enough to erupt a volcano of mauve beachplum gunk into the field, for which the birds adored me. Then I ran in with stained hands to wash off the sourest of all sour slime, teasing my mother with threatening monster sounds, waving my fingers in front of her.

"Go vash those sticky paws. Ve got vork to do."

---

* You crazy one!

In the kitchen, the contents of the *panela* heated on a low fire, each cup of juice combined with a cup of sugar.

While the sweet, tart juice reached the boiling point, I sat at the table and waited the hideously long wait of she who anticipates. My mother and I talked about little things as she did the dishes. I, of course, asked far too many times if it was ready.

She said, "Ach, for cryin' out loud, have a little patience. Everything comes to those who vait." When I could wait no longer, I ran outside to see if the yard smelled of the jelly. The scent permeated the kitchen air gradually, but outside the smell was stronger because it contrasted with the ocean breeze. When I had a nose full, I returned, and sure enough, she was turning down the fire so the jelly would simmer. That was the beginning of the true test.

My mother used a wooden spoon to scoop some of the simmering brew onto a saucer. Mostly she skimmed off the froth from the edges of the pot, a little of the juice gathering in the spoon with it. And there it was, the most inspiring of colors. Contemporary fashion mavens would call it "raspberry," but on the Vineyard, it's beachplum pink.

Maybe I loved the color for the late summer event it brought to mind. Maybe I loved it because it was bright and dramatic, or maybe because it was so significantly different than the dull navy blue and brown plaids of everything I wore. As with all things one loves, the reasons were probably many.

After the froth had time to cool, my mother held the saucer vertically over the simmering pot. A smidgen of jelly juice sneaked out from under the sticky froth and spilled across the saucer, dripping back into the pot.

"Not yet?" I'd whine, even though I knew the first five or six samplings would not pass the test.

"No, Miss Impatience. Not yet."

And I settled down to wait it out. A number of times she swept the pink froth onto the saucer. As my mother held the saucer above the pot, the not-thick-enough juice slid off again and again from under the froth that clung to the saucer. Finally, as she held it up for the last time, the congealed beach-plum juice slowly slid down the face of the saucer and gathered at the edge; no drips this time, but a triangular sail of translucent beachplum jelly hanging between the plate and the pot.

When she hugged me and said, "Vell, mein Susie, ve got ourselves some beautiful shelleè this year," I buried my face in her flowered apron and drank up the smells of salt air and sweet, tart beachplum jelly mist that clung to her.

The click of the gas stove signaled the next step and she handed me the saucer. At last! My mouth was aswamp with expectation, my taste buds screaming, "Yes, yes, yes!"

As I smeared the froth and new jelly over the piece of sweet-buttered rye bread that had nearly dried out with the wait, my mother ladled the piping hot jelly into the jars.

It always tasted the same, simultaneously tart and sweet, a taste like no other. In the middle of the ladling she came over and said, "Ach, let me taste that vonderful stuff! You're a lucky kid, mein Susie, to have a mother that cooks so good! Ach, I'm my own best customer!" and she licked her fingers with a resounding smack of the lips.

When the thirty or so jars were full, and the pot and utensils were flung in the double-wide enamel sink all in a clatter, she broke up a tablet of paraffin into a special little pot that was, from year to year, used for no other purpose. The burbling of the melting paraffin intrigued me enough to prompt repeated warnings about getting too close.

When she poured the liquid wax onto the cooling jelly, I knew each time that *this* was the time that the two would marry and mingle. I was wrong every time. Having heard one final maternal edict not to "mess vith my shelleè," I knelt on a chair to watch the wax harden white exactly the same size and shape of each jar mouth.

Before we stored the jars of jelly on the unheated back porch to become gifts for each departing visitor over the next three seasons, my mother would hold up not one or two but *every* jar in the sunlight of the kitchen window.

She'd say, "Look at that, mein Susie. Can you see that little ruby vindow right there in the middle? Ach! Vhat a vonderful thing, a beachplum!"

Fanny

WHEN FANNY ARRIVED for her annual two week vacation on the Vineyard, the windows flew open and the sun streamed in.

She had emigrated from Vienna years before and lived in Worcester, on the mainland, but each year she spent part of July with us.

Each morning I tiptoed halfway down the stairs, lured by the smell of fresh brewed Maxwell House. I hovered, listening for the "sk-sk, sk-sk" of her slippers on the linoleum, fully descending only when I heard the clink of the silverware and the sound of her package of Rye Krisp opening. It meant my place was set and she was ready to talk over breakfast.

She wore a full-length flannel nightgown even though it was July, with her shiny black braid hanging nearly down to her waist. She was the only woman her age I knew that did not have gray hair.

She spread two pieces of rye bread with butter and my mother's homemade jelly and put them on a small white plate with one pink rose painted on it. Next to it stood a cup of coffee with sugar and enough milk to make it just the right temperature for me to drink. Fanny scraped a mist of unsweetened butter across a rectangle of Rye Krisp and took tiny bites.

Every day she offered me a piece of Rye Krisp. But I was afraid it would cause my teeth to make the staccato clack at the back of my mouth the way hers did. So I remained uninitiated in the joys of a breakfast meant to keep one regular.

She always slurped her coffee, for boiling hot was the only way she drank it. In between slurps and clacks, she asked me questions unlike the questions other adults asked. A breakfast conversation with Fanny McGrath meant a little girl had to remember her dreams from the night before as well as from the eleven months since their last visit.

The best thing about Fanny asking a question was that she paid attention to the answer. She had the darkest eyes I had ever seen. They encompassed me and all that I told as if she were building pictures of the things I described. I usually saved my tales of the images I saw until she arrived.

But I had been so taken with one of the sky images I had seen several months before that I had told the family about it before Fanny's arrival. My wonder was greeted with the amused laughter of folks wondering how this imaginative little bird landed in this particular nest. I misunderstood their laughter and promised that I would keep my images secret.

Fanny coaxed me ever so gently, promising not to laugh. So I told her about having seen a huge smiling white-bearded man in the clouds with a cloak that reached all the way to town. She asked me what he had said. I was so stunned that she knew he had spoken I forgot to check to see if she had laughed. I leaned over and whispered, "He said, 'I'm with you always.'"

Fanny said nothing. But she looked at me with a sweet smile for a very long time.

We spent wonderful days together winding my mother's yarn off the skeins into big squishy spheres, drawing pictures, and taking long walks up Wing Road to gather bouquets of big flat elderberry blossoms.

We kept the flowers in the icebox (as my mother always called it) until the next morning when Fanny made big thin pancakes and plopped the whole blossom upside-down in the baking powder bubbles before she flipped them over. The thinness of the pancake provided a translucent hint of the fire-work-shaped flower trapped inside. I loved them. But the sight of them made my sister Eleanor's facial features distort into an immensely disapproving grimace. So I got to eat them all.

After breakfast each day, Fanny disappeared for a short while. When she came downstairs again her braid had become a bun at the nape of her neck. She was dressed in either a white dress with a tiny dark blue print, or a navy blue dress with a white fleck pattern, serious blue shoes, and shiny silver and blue earrings that I loved.

The summer I would be five, our family was breaking up. I wasn't aware of that. I only knew that there was a shadow I didn't understand in the eyes of everyone I loved. When Fanny arrived for her annual visit, she distracted me with her attention and challenging conversations.

While she was there that summer, we had the most dramatic thunderstorm I can remember. My mother, deathly afraid of lightning, was fleeing the windowed rooms, her raised arms waving in the air, as she said over and over in her most impassioned tones, "Ach du lieber Gott im Himmel! Ach du lieber Gott im Himmel!" She was German to the core every minute of every day. But she was German to the tenth power when a thunderstorm hit.

Being the instructive mother that she was, she modeled fear of thunderstorms so well that I too was frantic when one rumbled across the skies. I was looking for a place to hide when she grabbed a pillow off the couch as she flew by, heading for the upstairs bedrooms, where she yanked the shades down in one fell swoop. She then ran back down the stairs, plopped herself down on the fourth step from the bottom, closed and locked the door at the foot of the stairs, wrapped the pillow around her face to block out the sound and light of the storm, and continued her muffled litany of "Ach du lieber Gott im Himmel!" This was standard and quite acceptable thunderstorm behavior in our house.

But the "dear God in heaven" upon whom she called was busy causing an unbelievable ruckus that rattled and shook our very existence that day.

I was bouncing back and forth across the living room, so agitated by the storm that I couldn't center myself enough to find a place where I thought I would be safe.

"We're going for a walk," Fanny said. *That* stopped me in my tracks, as she knew it would. I looked at her, totally shocked that she would suggest such a stupid thing, and realized by the look on her face that she was not playing with me. I gave her a quick, succinct rundown of the perils of being out of doors in a storm. I had heard them so often that for me, at almost five years old, they were scripted lines.

"I know your mama believes those things. But I do not. Will you come with me?" She held out a hand.

What a dilemma! Do I stay safe and sound, heeding the storm-watch lament of the mother I adore? Or do I hold the hand of this woman whom I also adore and let her march me straightaway into the storm? The choice was easier than I thought. I trusted Fanny. Didn't she predict many, many years ago that my mother would have a third child late in life? And wasn't I standing there? Didn't she understand my night dreams and ask me questions that made me remember more? Could she be wrong about the storm?

"I'll get my coat," I whispered.

"No coats," Fanny said, "and take off your shoes." I was stunned. This went against all the rules of storm preparation my mother had drilled into me, along with staying away from the telephone, not sleeping in a metal bed, and unplugging every electrical appliance, lamp and radio in the house. In spite of that, I prepared to march into the storm, perhaps to my death. We took off our shoes together, and placed them side by side near the front door, my brown oxfords and her navy blue laced pumps.

Then, hand in hand, a little pigtailed four-year-old in black pants and red plaid short-sleeved shirt, and a sixty-year-old woman wearing a white short-sleeved shirtdress with dark blue print and blue earrings, stood on the front steps. Above, the storm slashed and roared.

Barefoot in the warm rain, we strolled out from under our maple tree while the rain pounded the leaves so hard we couldn't hear each other. And so we walked in silence, drenched and warm, the lightning illuminating the whole world, the yellow-gray air vibrating with thunder that ripped the sky, stealing my heartbeat. I was petrified! But we kept on walking, fat raindrops blapping on the part in my hair, gathering loose hairs into meandering streams down across my face.

I clutched her whole forearm with both my arms. We walked up Wing Road, totally alone. The traffic in 1956 was nothing to speak of. But in this storm, what people there were had pulled over to the side to wait it out, their inadequate windshield wipers at a standstill.

Fanny and I sloshed through the storm, so much water in the roadside river that it swirled around our ankles, gushing up and hiding our feet. When we had walked the full length of Norris Avenue and down the hill of Vineyard Avenue to the fire barn we called simply "number four," we turned right on Dukes County Avenue and headed back to Wing Road.

The thunder fell behind the lightning, and the storm headed out to sea. The rain continued, but more gently. The sky, dark and ominous above, held a hopeful band of lighter gray on the horizon.

It was then we could hear each other again, and Fanny began.

She spoke of my little world and my island and of the wider world, and of the worlds we cannot see. She told me of the great workings of the universe. "Beyond all of what you can see, even the moon and stars which are so very far away, beyond all that, the universe is made up of only one thing, and that is love."

She said that sometimes we human beings get too settled into ourselves and forget how great the universe is and how tiny a part we each are, but a part nonetheless. She spoke of the delicious days on the island when the wind is out of the southwest and the air lies soft on your cheek, and about the days of high drama in the heavens when the thunder and lightning play out their song. She said, "Even though we are right here in the middle of the storm, the sun is shining above the clouds." She spoke of darkness and light, not as opposites, but as two parts of a whole, one nonexistent without the other. She said, "The stars, and the moon and sun, each of them, like you, is part of an immense and endless dance."

She looked at me then, her face very serious, and said, "There will be times of great darkness, and the world around you will be full of frightening noise. Sometimes the storm is in the sky, and sometimes it can be in your own house. The thunder and lightning will surround everything. But you must remember, Susie, that surrounding the storm, above it and below it, before it and after it, there is love. Fear can be like a magnet, it is so strong. But love is the most powerful force in the universe."

It was my very first conversation about the cosmos. We walked home in silence, the new ideas swirling in my head like leaves in a whirlpool. Every other step I made a huge splash and watched the flying raindrops rejoin the flood racing to the sea.

When Fanny walked and I swaggered back across the lawn, I was no longer holding her hand. A car went by, slowing down to a crawl as its driver gazed unbelieving at what my mother would soon call "two drowned rats the cat dragged in." The shush of the tires in the flooded street and the rap of the rain from the roof pattering on the propane tanks softened as we walked into the house.

My mother was a nervous wreck, certain that we had been fried by the lightning. She said, "Ach, du lieber Gott im Himmel!" once more and flung her arms around us. "Ach, Fanny, bist du verrückte?* Are you trying to kill my kid?"

She brought some towels and dried us off, then wrenched some dry clothes onto my pruney skin. The towels sopped up everything except for the rivulet that streamed from the snail of braid at the nape of Fanny's neck.

With exasperation, my mother said, "Vhat in the name of heaven vere you two doing in that storm? I thought I'd die of fear."

It was then that I had my *second* conversation about the cosmos, regaling my mother with my new understanding of darkness and light.

After Fanny left that summer, our family fulfilled another of her predictions. My parents would not live out their lives together. Fanny had said so, long before I was born.

Having Fanny there had been a high time for me because I was never the same when she left. She was a blossom who left

* Fanny, are you crazy?

yet another petal with me each year.

As the summers came and went, we saw less and less of Fanny. She finally did not come at all, having died of cancer in the spring of the year. I missed her and her unique perspective on things seen and unseen for a long time.

The Flying Horses

IN 1835, A GROUP OF METHODISTS sailed to Martha's Vineyard to celebrate the glory of their maker while camping in the woods of Oak Bluffs. They enjoyed it so much that they began returning year after year to what is now "The Campgrounds,"* eventually building wooden frames for their tent canvas, creating temporary homes that resembled tiny cloth cathedrals. Over time, they closed in the frames and hung real doors, providing a buffer against weather and the prying curiosity of their fellow worshipers.

Architecturally, the period encouraged the ornate. So with lathes and imagination, the houses became studies in visual whimsy. Nestled close together in a huge circle on forty acres encompassing central public grounds, each house sported a different design of carved wooden gingerbread along roofline and porch rail. Etched cherry-red windowpanes of sandwich glass crowned each of the many clear gothic windows.

Outside the circle of fairy tale houses, smaller roundels and intertwining paths were lined with houses even smaller, with a tendency toward simpler ornamentation.

---

* formally referred to as the Martha's Vineyard Campmeeting Association

It was to one of these that I moved with my mother and sister when our family broke up, leaving my father at home on Wing Road. Unpainted and completely devoid of embellishment, ours was the lone gingerbread house without frosting, and, as the winter proved, without insulation.

The gunmetal sky hung low that miserably cold winter, and the snow just kept on falling. I stood in the park by Trinity Church studying the way the windblown flakes had settled in the nooks and curves of the brightly painted lathe work of the empty summer houses. As the sky cleared, the glistening of the snow made the bold colors sparkle in contrast. When the damp cold had finally penetrated my jacket, I warmed myself by copying the swirl and point of the woodwork in my footprint designs in the porch snow. The summer inhabitants never knew that the restful place where they rocked and swatted mosquitoes was actually the glistening white palette for the "soft-shoeing" winter boots of a five-year-old. The whorls of my designs were broken by the dark stripes where the snow had fallen through wide cracks between the porch boards.

In a summer resort, the hush of winter provides even a child the opportunity to think the quieter thoughts. All that I saw was frozen in place except for the rare red ribbon of a path cut by a swooping cardinal. Since less than a dozen of the hundreds of houses were occupied off-season, all else was at a standstill.

In the middle of the big circle of houses, there stands a huge and quite beautiful iron framework tabernacle. Its stained glass windows are situated on a short high wall separating two tiers of round corrugated roofs. Throughout the day, the sun sends its colorful reflections in a measured waltz across the wooden benches below. The high hollow dome is a perfect receptacle for a child's voice flung into the air. Its metal roof absorbs no sound, but rather bounces the waves back, magnified but muffled in the great curve of tin.

It was a good place to spend some time each day testing the response of the building to whispers and shouts. Tiring of that, I wandered about the town. I had pretty much free rein of Oak Bluffs, the parts that I knew anyway. Both my mother and sister worked all day, and because I was only old enough for a half-day of kindergarten, I was blessed with an informal babysitting situation. As long as I checked in with "Aunt" Martha, next door, a woman with the tiniest but coziest kitchen ever built, I could pretty much go where I pleased.

My daily ritual was to get dressed and put the dime I had been saving since the end of summer in my pants pocket, just in case this was the day I would find somewhere to spend it. Everything had shut down on Labor Day except for the post office, Phillips's Hardware Store, Pacheco's Grocery Store, the 5 & 10, and the Red and White, another grocery store whose produce section was bordered by the squeakiest wooden floors I had ever had the pleasure to bounce on.

So, aside from the Campgrounds' mazelike paths where, incredibly, I never got lost, there were only two places I cared to visit.

The beach in winter is a pale, lonely strand. But with the gentle rhythmic shushing of the waves on a windless day, I frolicked with mermaids and buccaneers and all manner of sea creatures. In between my visits with them, I gathered sea glass. These wonderfully smooth old shards of broken glass had been tossed over the sides of docks and boats and pirate ships in near or far-off places and miraculously transported to the very place I was standing.

Edges dulled and surfaces frosted by the action of rolling rocks and moving sand and water, the sea glass was a treasure, I thought, for its texture alone. Olive greens from champagne bottles and brown from beer, and white from clear bottles and jars were most certainly the commoners in the sea glass world. But the transformed blue fragments so hard to come by were the royalty. Perhaps they were shards of former Noxema jars or from Milk of Magnesia or Evening in Paris perfume. Whatever the source, a piece of cobalt sea glass was a rare and highly prized possession, and I was usually apportioned only one a year by the great sea.

Empty scallop shells, tiny and perfect, washed up on shore, their meat slurped up by deep-bellied sea gulls. I harvested glass and shells until my pockets bulged with treasure. Before heading home, I paid a visit to one of Oak Bluffs' sweetest spots.

Our town is proud of its Flying Horses, the "oldest operating carousel in the nation," though as a child I didn't know it was the oldest, nor would I have cared. Before geography lessons and off-island travel enlightened us, we children assumed that all people lived as we did. So we thought the world was made up of islands, each having its own merry-go-round. What a pity we were wrong.

In a not-so-very-large tongue and groove building with faded yellow paint and bent iron pipe railings at opposite entrances, situated on a triangle of asphalt in the center of town, a beautiful herd of horses rode round and round during the summer season. On Labor Day, the horses became unavailable to island children whose desires did not always coincide with the tourist calendar.

But when the Flying Horses was open, the doors stood wide and the wooden shutters were unhooked daily, their enormous boards pushed out and up and fastened by long hooks that slid into strong metal eyes. Light flooded the carousel and salt-laden breezes swooped in from the ocean, which lay just beyond the old Tivoli building, center of dances and wrestling matches during the soft season. The wooden shutters covered the upper half of a huge wall where glass windows and screens could have been.

For five minutes or so, the dizzying spin on stationary wooden horses propelled us to distant realms. Most of us did not have flesh and blood horses of our own, so it took little stimulus to lift us out of our mundane have-not world into the shining land where all is possible. Popcorn popped and pink cotton candy spun its sweetness into the air next to the ticket booth where eager children waited, the littlest bouncing up and down, up and down with excitement on the oily old wooden floor.

As soon as we were up on the horses, Mr. Hastings pulled twice on the leather thong that rang the brass bell. In one motion, his left arm pushed down the big brass-handled lever that spun the huge turntable on which we galloped, while his right pulled him up onto the carousel floor with a creak and a sag of the whole mechanism. Traveling against the rush of the herd, he pulled himself from horse to horse, holding on to the metal rods that held them in place. Collecting little yellow tickets from each child, he stopped for a moment by the red leather chariots that separated the groups of horses to chat with parents along for the ride. The ching-a-ching of the steel rings sliding into each other as they rolled down the bright red ring arm, which swiveled into place as the ride began, continued until the brass ring (which we called the "gold" ring) was put in near the end of the ride after a nod to the "ring boy" from Mr. Hastings.

Older kids and especially teenagers with long arms who stood next to the little kids' horses yanked three or four, sometimes even five rings out of the brass-covered business end of the ring arm by reaching far forward as they approached the rings, and then reached so far back arms nearly popped out of sockets. Rings flew all over the place, rolling this way and that like inebriated little spirals, finally landing between the feet of the people waiting for the next ride. While riding, the ring catchers dropped their handfuls of rings onto metal spindles growing out of the top of the horses' heads, accumulating testimony to a capable hand. When the spindle was full, the rings were flung into the huge red leather ring box on the back wall approaching the ring arm. With a fluid rhythm, you could remove the whole batch of rings, appearing as if you were going to throw them into the box. But on the way to the box you could let one or two fly out the huge windows, hoping no one was walking by at just that moment. The rest of the rings flew into the box, and no one was the wiser. The rings were outside to collect on the way home. Some kids had shoe boxes full. Mr. Hastings surely must have guessed the reason for the constant need to resupply. But as far as I know, he never said a word to anyone, and he never bothered to screen in the huge openings.

It was there I went almost daily, to sit on the snowy steps and wait for spring. Occasionally a car drove by, traveling from Beach Road. But other than that I was pretty much alone, and as usual on the Vineyard, spring was a reluctant visitor. I sat until the cold overtook me and I had to move in order to keep breathing.

One day as I waited there, Mr. Hastings appeared. He looked exactly the way he did in summer, except a winter jacket covered the red plaid shirt I was sure he must have been wearing. Khaki pants and gold wire-rimmed glasses finished the familiar picture.

"What on earth are you doing here, Susie?" he asked.

"I'm waiting for spring!" I said with great hope that it might have arrived without my knowing. "Is it here? Are the horses going to go around?"

"No, not for a long while. Easter weekend is a ways off yet. Come on in if you like. It'll be cold in there, though."

So I followed him. In winter, the inside of an uninsulated

building in New England holds the bone-chilling cold of all winters. It was much colder inside than out, and the poor horses were frozen in place. I just stood there watching them.

"Do you have a favorite?"

"Oh, yes! I do! It's the big black one* that stands up with his front legs in the air, the tallest one."

"Is it because you're so short that you like the tallest one?"

"No. I like the tallest one because he's the prettiest," I said matter-of-factly.

I was looking straight at that horse and he was looking straight back at me. The horse's glass eye had a tiny lead animal figurine inside that made the horse's gaze able to follow me as I walked by.

I said again, "Are the horses going anywhere today?"

"No, not today."

I thought that was too bad, because I had put that dime in my pocket that morning, just like every morning, just in case. And this looked like the perfect place to spend that dime, now pulsing in my pocket, the exact price of a ticket.

Finally, after we talked for awhile and he busied himself with whatever tasks he came to do, he said, "You know, Susie, I'm looking at these horses and they're looking mighty stiff. I think they need some exercise. You like the Blue Danube Waltz?"

I said, "Mm hmm! I *love* the Blue Danube Waltz!" Every kid in town knew the strains of the Blue Danube since it was

---

* An historical refurbishing of the merry-go-round has recently been completed. The black horse is now returned to its original dappled brown.

the only song the carousel played.

So he climbed up onto the rickety platform where the horses ran wild in warmer weather and headed for the hub. Through a slit in a red leather panel of the hub, he flipped a switch. It felt like the whole building might come to life, such was the grinding and whirring from deep within. He hoisted me up onto that big black horse and strapped me in with the old belt of cracked brown leather that was attached to the saddle.

I said, "I have my dime! I've been saving it since last summer!" I dug it out and placed it flat in his palm. When he pushed the big lever, the Blue Danube began to play, and I rode the merry-go-round alone, leading the herd round and round.

The hub of the carousel was paneled with full-length paintings. With shining stares, the mermaid, the cowboy, and Neptune with his trident invited me on one journey after another. The panel of the steamboat beckoned, promising a voyage to anywhere I chose. Above the long panels were pastorals, small four-cornered lures of fantasy, and suspended from each spoke of the actual structural armature overhead were small distinctive landscapes, each pulling the eye and spirit forward and farther into another world. Riding those horses was a commitment to journey, the scenery only limited by the speed of my mind's eye.

During that fragment of the Blue Danube, scores of lifetimes could be lived. When the music ended and the spinning stopped, Mr. Hastings said, "Those horses really did need some limbering up! I'm so glad you were here to help me. Thanks for taking them round. But I have to close up now because I've errands to do today." He lifted me off the horse while it still pawed the air and set me down on the floor.

"Thanks so much for letting me ride!"

"You're very welcome. See you in the spring, Susie!"

"Yeah! You will!" and I was out the door, filled with the joy of having ridden the merry-go-round all alone in winter. Almost as sweet would be the telling about it.

With the music in my head and a huge grin on my face, I was off to the beach to see what else I could find on my way home. But finding that I had already scavenged up every last shell and bit of sea glass, I climbed the stairs up from the beach and cut across Ocean Park, sliding across the ice on the shallow turquoise cement pond where toy sailboats bobbed in summer. I cut through the narrow yards between the big silent houses rimming the park and headed through the arch of the Arcade and back into the Campgrounds.

In Aunt Martha's kitchen I dug down into my pockets to take everything out. As usual, she sat at the table with me as I sorted the shells and glass by size, color, and shape. I told her all about my trip to the Flying Horses and what happened inside. She smiled a grin almost as big as mine and told me I was one lucky little girl.

When I thought I had pulled everything out I felt one more shell at the bottom. As I was pulling it out, my fingers recognized the cool, familiar surface of something I had carried for a long time. It was my dime.

Jaeger's House

IT WAS WHEN WE LIVED at Jaeger's house in the Campgrounds that I discovered the "six-year-old-little-girl-eating" wolf that lived at the top of the parlor staircase. No one in the family mentioned the wolf, so I didn't either. We didn't use the parlor because it faced northeast and the house wasn't winterized. We were cold enough in the rest of the house, where we huddled together, keeping the oil man rich.

I usually encountered the wolf when I used the only bathroom in the house, in the front hall at the top of the stairs. I never saw him, only greeted him, sticking out my tongue in mock bravery, jumping over the two stairs that led from bathroom to hallway, fleeing to the stairs shouting, "You'll never catch me!" as I vaulted my tiny self up onto the banister and slid down a hundred miles an hour, flipping one leg over at just the right time to avoid shattering my pelvis on the huge wooden post at the end, touching down on the very last step, and flying through that frigid dead-air parlor to the safety and warmth of the dining room we used for a living room. My mother asked why I was always out of breath after going to the toilet.

The winter was hideous there, miserably cold, the wind always blowing through the uninsulated wooden walls. We were struggling to keep our spirited heads above water, my mother, my sister and I. Our family, newly divorced, had traded old hardships for new ones, none of which I would recommend.

There were very few highlights that winter. There was a rose-colored room directly above the parlor. We didn't use it either because of the northeast wind. I was told to stay out of there.

What better invitation! I stole up the back stairs, cut through the back bedrooms, and marched through the front hall since the wolf slept all day. Then, quietly turning the knob, I let myself into the most exciting place I had ever been. I hopped up onto the satiny rose bedspread, as slippery and cold as ice, and lay my head back in the pillows and stared straight ahead at the dark rose walls. Across from the mahogany bed, on the wall facing the harbor, were two wonderful pictures. I'd never seen anything like them and could not believe someone even thought of painting a ballerina and a matador in bright colors on black velvet, an incredible sight to behold for a six-year-old so cloistered she had not yet seen her first magazine.

I lay there staring until they came to life.

She wore pink, of course, effortlessly twirling and pirouetting across the black velvet, one delicately poised hand held high above her.

He wore black adorned with silver braid and bravely

swung his crimson cape in a figure eight, enticing a bull that never had the courage to approach him.

Each time I came to watch them, it was always the same. They faced away from one another, she staring into ballerina space, he focusing on the flutter of the cape. But I could tell they were secretly looking at one another. Each danced the dance of approach. But neither could dance beyond the velvet frame. No matter how hard I willed them to reach for each other, they would not, could not. Frozen nearly stiff, my imprint still in the shiny spread, I closed the door softly on the rose-colored room.

When spring finally came, I was outdoors with my dolls all the time. Our house had two porches, a large one attached to the parlor and a tiny one attached to the dining room, both facing northeast. Because the house was in the Campgrounds where all the houses are literally inches apart and delightfully covered with gingerbread trim, we had absolutely no front yard and only a small backyard.

So I played island visitor with my dolls. We wintered on the tiny porch, the dolls bundled up in all the blankets I had while they wore all their clothes to keep warm—all except the little tan dress with the pale pink roses on it that disappeared when I had dressed a reluctant neighborhood cat in it. The last I had seen of that dress, it was flying out of my doll carriage around the torso of a furious and uncomfortable feline that yowled, stumbled, and peed as she fled. Getting her into the dress had not been an easy task. I can't imagine what brave soul got her out of it.

Once my dolls were warm and snugly, I reassured them all the time that summer would soon arrive, and we could once again travel to our summer island house. I sang to them the whole winter long and told them stories of the ballerina and the matador.

When I felt spring in the air, I removed all the dolls' clothes and blankets, packed up the winter house for the season, and rattled my two-tone green doll carriage down the steps and across the broken macadam to the front porch, our summer residence. Of course, it was much bigger, just like all the big summer homes up on the bluff at East Chop. I even had an old wicker chair at the summer cottage in which I rocked my dolls to sleep, which they sorely needed after being dragged and clunked upstairs backwards in the carriage.

We lived there, whiling away the summer for part of a day. I danced and sang for them until the leaves started to fall. Then I packed it up again and trundled my doll children back to the winter porch once more. Years passed every day in the course of my biannual migrations.

Late that spring I was on the winter porch when I heard my father softly calling me. I was surprised to see him standing in the backyard. It was rare that he visited me though he still lived in our old house about half a mile away. I was singing to my favorite doll, "Frenchie," as I rocked her to sleep in my arms. I had no wicker chair on the winter porch.

Still holding Frenchie, I went to meet my father in the back yard. I wanted to run up into his arms, hold him for a long time, and then take a ride on his shoulders the way I used to.

But he looked so tired, I didn't think his arms would hold me if I leapt into them.

He whispered to me that no one should know he was there. He said he was moving away from the island and had come to say goodbye. I just stood there and he just stood there. I could feel the widening of the dark hole that had come to live in my heart, and I held Frenchie closer to keep the fear from bursting my heart to pieces. We stood there for so long looking down but looking at each other. I wanted him to grab me up and hold me. I didn't know then that if he had, he would never have been able to go. He told me he loved me and then turned away. I looked at him then. I looked at him hard. I wanted to say something, to cry. But I wouldn't, I couldn't. So I watched the back of him as he walked away, his hands in his pockets, his shoulders slumped, the knife-blade creases of his khaki pants behind each knee, one then the other. I watched until the creases carried him away.

I told no one that he had come to see me. Nothing really changed. My dolls and I still lived our summers and winters porch to porch every day. But the wolf at the top of the stairs threatened no longer. And the ballerina and the matador never danced towards each other again.

Blood Kin

MY FIRST BICYCLE had been found at what we called the Warehouse, the town dump. It was a tiny one, black with white stars and handle grips, and training wheels on the back that could be lifted up. But I wasn't ready for that. The bicycle and I were made for each other size wise and I pedaled my little heart out. I loved the freedom it brought. Now, I could really go places. The bike gently rocked as the training wheels touched the road on either side … back and forth, back and forth … providing a needed security in my venturing.

I'd had the bike for a few weeks when my best friend and nemesis, David Amaral, said, "Come on! We're taking those training wheels off today. I'll hold the fender while you ride. You can do it!" Mutual discussion before decision-making was something David never considered.

He lived two doors up the street from me on Wing Road. We were the same age but for eight months that he used for every ounce of leverage it was worth. We had played together since we were toddlers.

Even now, David will tell anyone who mentions my name, "Oh, yeah, Susan sure is a know-it-all. And it's true, she knows everything. And everything she knows, I taught her." The truth is, he did teach me to ride that bike.

He was right behind me, pulling the training wheels up as he held the fender. He talked a mile a minute (something for which he is still noted), to keep my mind off what was really happening. "Come on, Klein, you can do it! You don't need those sissy wheels anymore. Just hold on and concentrate. Don't forget to watch where you're going. You wanna fly? Stick with me!"

He ran, holding the fender steady as I pedaled as fast as I could. When he stopped talking the only sound was the wind making a "flacka-flacka" noise through the cast-off handle grip streamers David had given me. When I discovered I was really riding on my own because he had let go, I fell off, solely from the shock of independence. From then on, I rode not with four wheels but with two. I felt I could go to the ends of the earth, the fact that we lived on an island notwithstanding.

One day, he said, "You're gonna ride *my* bike today." While I protested that the bike was way too big for me, we walked to his house. He turned a bushel basket upside down so I could climb up on it. Otherwise I would not have been able to reach the seat as it was one of those twenty-six inch skinny-tired jobs, and I was very short.

I said, "David, I don't think my legs are long enough!"

He said, "They're long enough. Get on!"

Believing David was my first mistake. Getting on the bike was the second. But I had longed to ride David's shiny red bike since he got it for Christmas, and this was the very first time he had offered to let me use it.

It was my first time on a normal bike in a while, for by this time my little starry bike was broken. Big Steve, the kid up the road, about four years older than us, had ridden it one day and snapped off the left pedal flush with the frame. I was horrified at the sight. But I continued to ride that bicycle one-pedaled, my left leg stuck straight out in the wind, my right foot twisted at an uncomfortable angle against the lone pedal to create the resistance needed to stay upright.

So David was being quite generous letting me ride his new bike. When he got me propped up on the seat, my little legs strained to reach the pedals.

My voice was unheeded by David as he pushed me out of the driveway directly across Wing Road, unheeded as my objection, "I don't think this is going to ..." trailed in the breeze. I managed to miss whatever traffic there was as I coasted at a mighty smart clip down Franklin Avenue, which connects Wing Road with what is fondly called "Chicken Street." Its legal name is Vineyard Avenue. Rumor has it that all town gossip that isn't spawned at Town Hall originates from the cackling hens down there, hence the name, "Chicken Street." But then where was that rumor born?

It was clear I was going to reach Chicken Street right soon and hit either a telephone pole or an oncoming car. So I tried to "think" my legs longer to get enough pressure to put on the brakes. The pedals spun backwards wildly, making a high-pitched whine, accomplishing nothing but heightened panic. David had neglected to mention that this bike had hand brakes.

As I careened down Franklin, I spied the barn on the corner of Forest Hill Avenue, which triggered some memory of a lesson involving a body in motion meeting a body at rest. So I aimed the bike at the barn, smashed head-on into a nicely placed bale of hay, and landed with the bicycle on top of me. I struggled for a while in the hay to get the death chariot off me and then walked it home.

I came puffing up the hill, my arms stretched up above my head to reach the handlebars. This time I could look left, right, left before crossing Wing Road. Hay sticking out of my clothes and hair, I pushed the bike at David, who stood in the driveway wearing the slyest of grins.

"Didn't work out too good, huh, Klein?"

I knew a setup when I saw one. I vowed to learn to recognize the next one before I became its victim. I also swore I'd never speak to David again.

But of course, with the engaging smile and alluring charm of a con artist, David made sure we were best friends by morning. We watched a cowboy movie on TV and made a promise not to fight anymore; a promise to do the impossible. Instead we would seal our friendship with blood.

In the backyard, David opened his jackknife, and we slit the soft pillows on the outside of our right palms. Wincing from the incisions, we pressed the dripping cuts together for a long time until we were certain we had become blood brother and sister.

Our blood dried on our hands as we sat in the grass and

talked about everything we would do for the rest of our lives and we would do it only one way, we said, just like in the TV westerns, like The Lone Ranger and Tonto, like Cisco and Pancho, we'd do it together.

The wounds healed, trapping us inside each other, and we remained entwined, though not as serenely as we had vowed. When we were ten, David's father and my sister got married. Becoming David's aunt distanced us in some unspoken and confusing way, as if, as children, we were really expected to assume those roles. We had become family in a way that was not immediately comfortable. I hated being called "Aunt Susie" by townspeople and classmates who thought it fun to tease me. Outwardly, our new relationship had redefined us, but it could not overcome the bond we felt as blood kin.

Making Ends Meet

IN MY MOTHER'S HOUSE there is a place at the top of the stairs to sit undiscovered and listen to conversations in the kitchen. During the year that I turned seven, I sat up there a good deal while the family thought I was in bed, asleep. My sister Eleanor and her friend Gerry Sylvia would sit with my mother and try to make sense of the world. There were stories of who was doing what with whom, the seasonal discussions of opening and closing the houses of summer people, along with the range of complaints and joys brought on by the current weather.

But the intrigue for me was in trying to understand so much talk of not being able to "make ends meet." I spent an inordinate amount of time trying to figure out, "the ends of *what?*" I imagined all sorts of things with gaps and someone trying desperately to bring them together.

When I finally understood the strange "making ends meet" business from piecing together months of conversations, I was terrified. It was the late 1950s and we lived on an island without a sustaining industry. Most people were struggling.

Just what did people do when they did not have enough money? One night I heard my mother say, "That'll send them to the poorhouse," during my eavesdropping session. So I figured we'd be packing any day to go live there. I didn't want to pack to go anywhere, least of all the poorhouse. Our family had gone through a divorce, and Eleanor, my mother, and I had recently returned to the house from which we had fled. It was *my* house again, and I wanted only to know that it would always be.

But what of "making ends meet?" I knew I had to do something to help, without anyone knowing that I was trying to contribute, because I wasn't supposed to know about this. If my mother and Eleanor wanted me to know, the subject would have come up in daytime conversation.

I didn't have any evening time to think alone, because I was too busy trying to find out what the latest scoop was as I monitored those kitchen conversations. I'd woken up more than once, shivering in a crumpled heap by the wall, having fallen asleep before I put myself back to bed.

The next day I went to the small clearing amidst the hundreds of branches composing the wall of lilacs between our property and the neighbor's. It was my secret place underneath a canopy of leaves that veiled me from the neighborhood. The sun dappled the clearing while I sat on my root chair to think.

I didn't know how to go about getting a job, and I was only seven. Who would hire a seven-year-old? I thought about selling something. But I didn't own anything more than my books, a green doll carriage, my dolls, and the blue and white doll's crib that my father had made me. None of that would "make ends meet."

I could pick up bottles on the roadside and redeem them. What a scheme! Jackie and I did that every day anyway when I went with him on his paper route. I just wouldn't get a Devil Dog or a root beer Popsicle in exchange for the five bottles I usually managed to accumulate by the time we got to Tony's Market. But I knew that a nickel a day was not going to pay the oil man or the electric company.

I was feeling pretty forlorn when I was struck by idea lightning. If we had no money to pay for heat and light, then surely we would not have enough money to buy new school clothes for me. No school clothes meant I couldn't go to school. I *adored* school! Not to go meant certain death. In order to go, I would have to fit into my first-grade clothes and it was already the end of the summer. So in order to do my part and help out the family, I decided not to grow. The beauty of the decision was that they wouldn't know. But they also would not have to spend money we didn't have in order for me to attend school.

Though I thought it a brilliant idea, I wasn't sure how one went about *not* growing. It was one of those things that happened without too much dwelling on it.

So I tried not eating. Not only would we save clothing money, but we would save money at the grocery store too. Starving was a pretty miserable experience, however. And my mother, a fabulous cook who expected people to eat her food, noticed *that* one right off the bat. If I wanted to do this business of helping secretly, I had to eat, but not much.

Another trip to the lilac bushes provided the answer: prayer. Nightly I lay in bed and prayed that I would not grow, but only after I had spied on the adult conversations. I begged and pleaded with God to keep me the same height and dress size forever. As God and I became more intimate, I decided our nightly visits would also be a good time to ask for a new blue bicycle.

Knowing that we had money problems prompted me to pray that the bicycle would miraculously drop out of the sky. I could see no other means for its arrival. I had had a tiny black bicycle with white stars that we had procured from the town dump. My friend David had taught me to ride and I loved the freedom it brought. When the bike was broken I rode it with just one pedal until I had outgrown it. There was that growing thing again.

A seven-year-old with no wheels is a sorry sight. So I continued to pray for a blue bicycle to appear just for me, Susie, who was not growing. What a perfect idea! The bicycle and I would stay the same size and remain together until I was a very old woman and chose a rocking chair over the bicycle.

September arrived, just as it does every year on the island, clear and crisp. My mother woke me up one morning which was unusual. In our house you ate when you were hungry and slept when you were tired. Getting woken up was rare unless you had a job or there was a thunderstorm. I was the only one without a job, so I was surprised to be yanked from sleep.

"Come on, you 'dirty stay up late,' " she said, using the family nickname for late-sleeping children, "it's time to go get you some new clothes for school!"

"I don't want any new clothes. I like my old ones," I said in a pout.

"They don't fit you anymore, Susie. You've grown over the summer."

"No, I haven't."

"You kleine meshuggench!* Of course you have! Now, up you go and get ready."

"I'm telling you, Mama, I didn't grow. If my clothes from last year still fit, do I have to get new ones?"

"Vell, I suppose not, not if you really can vear them a vhile longer. But you need something new for the first day, anyvay. And you need new shoes. Your toes are right at the end of those oxfords."

SHOES!

How could I have forgotten my feet would grow? I prayed only for my dress size to stay the same and not to get taller. And shoes were the most expensive thing of all! I couldn't believe I hadn't done an inventory of body parts before I started praying. I knew trying to get around this shoe thing was pure folly. My mother only wore hand-me-down shoes that never fit her right when she was a kid in wartime Germany. If she'd said it once, she'd said it a trillion times, "No kid of mine is ever going vithout proper shoes."

My plan had failed, or so I thought. In fact, the clothes

---
* Yiddish: little crazy one

from first grade actually did fit. I hadn't grown. So we only needed to get new underwear and shoes.

After we bought the new brown school shoes with the sturdy arches, my mother flung a curse at me. "Now you've got room to grow!" she said with great delight. I doubled up on the prayers after that.

Earnestly beseeching God seemed to work. By Christmas I had grown only enough to need new winter pants. But everything else still fit, sort of.

My friend, David, came over Christmas Eve day to help me decorate the living room picture window with sponges, paint, and stencils of holly leaves and bells. We discussed our Christmas wishes. For the hundredth time that month he told me he wanted a BB gun, and I told him I wanted a blue bicycle. When we were finished daubing with the sponges, we went outside to work on the snow fort we had been building with the other neighborhood kids. It was growing each day. We were working on the principle of the igloo, something we tried every winter. The most recent snowfall had finally provided us with snow of the right consistency, since this was the first time a snow fort ever held up more than a few hours. It was a big tunnel, cold and blue inside. We were thrilled that we actually had done it. We'd have worked through the night if the adults responsible for us hadn't been so responsible.

We played through twilight, until our parents called us in. David and I parted wishing each other BB guns and blue bicycles. When I got home, I plugged in the electric candles that graced each of the living room windows and lit the string of lights that made the sparkling little cardboard houses sitting in cotton snow on the picture windowsill spring to life. I plugged in the last string. Fat bulbs of red, blue, green, and yellow peeked out from between the beer steins on the shelf above the room partition. On my sister's record player, I played my favorite album, a selection of traditional German Christmas carols. I was trying to learn them in German even though I couldn't speak the language. I sang "Kling Glöckchen, Kling-a-ling-a-ling," over and over again as I settled in for a long evening on the floor in front of the Christmas tree. There is no question but that a special relationship exists between Germans and their Christmas trees. All the trees in our family were amazingly ethereal. Ours that year seemed to glow from within. A dreamy haze of angel hair encircled it, and each light had a perfect halo.

When I went upstairs that night, Eleanor and Gerry and my mother were still sitting in the living room talking. I skipped my eavesdropping since I figured I'd need every spare minute to pray. So I asked again for a blue bicycle all my own, knowing nothing short of a miracle would produce one.

Being the first one up next morning, I tiptoed down to the living room. My eyes wanted so much to see a blue bicycle that they did. I blinked a few times and rubbed my eyes. But when I touched the metallic blue fender of that Western Flyer, it didn't disappear. I was simply overwhelmed at the sight of a dream come true. I just stood there and stared at it.

When reality set in, I tried to wish the bicycle away harder than I'd wished to get it there. This was no miracle sent from above. This was my sister, Eleanor, saving money from her job at the phone company. This meant that she had made sacrifices to have this blue bicycle under the tree on Christmas morning.

I heard her come up behind me. She said, "Look at that! It's just what you wanted, isn't it?" as if she and Santa Claus didn't share a soul.

I closed my eyes, and clenched my teeth, and without turning to her I said it. It was a most difficult thing to say. But I said it.

"Take it back!"

She spun me around, incredulous. "I thought it was what you wanted!"

"I never said that. I never wanted a bicycle. I don't need any bicycle!"

She said, "Susie, that's all you've talked about since your little bike got broken. Why don't you want this bike?"

Her face was so full of pain and confusion that it hurt to look at her. I said, "Eleanor! Take it back! I don't want it."

"This doesn't make sense! Tell me why you don't want this bike?"

"I don't want it and I don't need it. Will you just take it back!"

She said, "All right. I'll call Mr. Billings at Western Auto and ask him to come pick it up today. You haven't ridden a bicycle in a long time, though. Why don't you take this one for a short ride, so I can at least tell him that it's a good bicycle and works well?"

I struggled with that one for awhile. It never occurred to me that Western Auto was closed on Christmas day, so I didn't catch the white lie. All I heard was, "... take a ride ..." I wanted more than anything to keep that bicycle. But I knew I couldn't keep it because it had cost more than money. So I said, "No," and the house fell into silence.

We sat down to breakfast. But the lump in my throat was so thick, I couldn't get anything down. The bicycle I had prayed to appear now made my life impossible. Now I prayed for it to disappear, but it wouldn't. So I stayed away from the living room.

Finally, Eleanor came back into the kitchen and said, "I'm going to call Mr. Billings at the store. Please, go take a ride so that I can tell him the bike works."

I recognized a "last chance" in those words. So I agreed. As we bundled up, my heart was thundering in my chest. Eleanor and I carried the bicycle outside. Nothing could contain my grin as I grabbed those white handle grips and pushed off with that first thrust of energy it takes to start you on your way.

Well, I did take a ride, and not a short one. I rode up Wing Road, across Norris Avenue until I took a right onto Vineyard Avenue and a left onto Pacific, to the school, down School Street, and through every circular Campgrounds neighborhood, and then out onto Dukes County Avenue and back up Wing Road to our house. Eleanor was waiting on the porch as I snapped the kickstand down. The end of it disappeared into the snow of the unplowed driveway. She said, "I thought you got lost. Where did you go?"

I said, "You can tell Mr. Billings the bike is fine. It handles real well in the snow." That was something I had heard my friend David's father say about a Jeep he had bought, and I wanted to sound like I knew what I was talking about.

I was up on the porch now. She said, "The bicycle can't be returned. The store won't take it back. You have to keep it. Do you suppose you could do that?"

I burst into tears, flung my arms around her, and choked, "But we can't make ends meet!" If I hadn't been crying so hard myself I would have laughed at the way each of those words became multi-syllabic through my sobs.

She said, "How do you know that?"

And out came the whole story of listening to the kitchen conversations and deciding not to grow, the shoes snag and the praying. I couldn't for the life of me understand why that would make her cry and laugh at the same time.

She bent down on her knee and took me by the shoulders so she could talk to me face to face. Wiping my tears away, she said, "OK. We've been having a tough time. But Mom and I are both working and things will be all right. I promise. But it's Christmas, and this is your Christmas present. Now get on that thing and take a ride like a girl who has her own bicycle."

I whispered, "Thank you! It's a beauty," in her ear and she hugged me so hard it hurt. Over her shoulder I saw my mother's shadow move in the hall by the kitchen, eavesdropping. I raced out the door then, and as I turned out of the driveway into the road, I looked back at my sister standing on the stairs, a look of fierce resolution on her proud face. Then I rode the best blue bicycle ever made to David's just two doors away to see if he wanted to take a bike ride in the snow. He showed me his new BB gun and promised to teach me how it worked.

We rode everywhere that day, but mostly down by the sea where the wind had made so many small drifts spiking across the shore road. I looked at a hundred things that day, sparkling in the winter sun, all of them with the new eyes of a girl on her brand-new metallic blue bicycle.

Nightcrawling

SPRING WAS UPON US, so it was time to think of fish. David and I made our plans to prowl the backyard for nightcrawlers, those huge, juicy worms used for bait. They slide up out of their holes on damp evenings, and every spring evening is damp if you live near the sea.

I carried an old coffee can while David tried to sneak out of the house with his father Nelson's huge fireman's light. Banging the big battery attached to it into every piece of furniture as we made our way to the back door caused Nelson to yell from the living room recliner, "Don't you kids drop that light!" His voice was sterner than usual. The light had a steel wire cage that protected the reflector and bulb. Considering the number of times we dropped it, I guess one could say the designer had foresight.

Aiming the beam at the ground, we searched for night-crawler-sized craters that circled the passageways from which they had exited the earth. Here and there, not far from the craters, the worms were just lying about. We gently lifted each worm into the coffee can. They weren't so very slimy as one might think. But they tried to shrink up and disappear when we caught them. That made handling them a little dangerous for the worms, since we occasionally dropped them on their heads.

I saw two worms overlapping, the collar-like protuberances of each linked to the other. I called David to show him. Since our last worm-hunting escapade a year before, he had discovered that the raised ribbed collars on the worms were their sexual organs. Finding two joined together stirred some pretty lively conversation. He told me exactly what it meant when we found two together. I was astounded! But then we found three of them in a heap, the collars all attached. *David* was astounded! The hunt and resulting capture of these worms we called "nightcrawling." To this day, that word still gives me pause.

Rats!

RUSTY, DAVID'S BIG, BLOND, sweet-faced golden retriever, was known in the neighborhood for his benevolent thievery. Folks around town always put out pans of leftovers for their own animals to eat. Backyards were safe from skunks because in the 1950s the Vineyard was completely free of the smelly little bandits; safe from skunks, but not safe from Rusty, who would go marauding after dark in search of cookware, littering the yard with his finds.

He clamped his jaw around the rim of a pan so that it would often fly up in front of him and fit him like a knight's helmet without eye holes. Blind inside the pot, his olfactories full of tantalizing Portuguese seasonings and linguica,* he found his way home nonetheless. We rarely saw him do it. But a headless dog in the dark sporting Revereware is not easily forgotten. Eleanor was always getting phone calls requesting a backyard check for lasagna pans and soup pots.

But for these foraging journeys, Rusty and David were inseparable. So when it was rat-killing time, which occurred every now and then, Rusty was always available for duty. The

---

* a Portuguese pork sausage heavily spiced with paprika

rats were occasionally a problem because Nelson, David's dad, and my sister Eleanor kept chickens, and rats *love* chickens.

I, however, do not. My first, last, and only trip into the chicken coop was my horrific introduction to David's vicious rooster who always attacked from the rear. Talons in the behind deter visits. I secretly hoped the rats would invade the chicken yard and head straight for the rooster en masse. But it never happened. The rooster was there every morning with that superior look in his eye.

When the rats did infest the coop, David's dad, perhaps the most verbally reserved man in Oak Bluffs, would find us and say in an ominous whisper, "Rats!"

Knowing what was coming, we crouched down to dog-ear level and with great expectancy whispered, "Hey, Rusty! RATS!" The word "rats" whispered just so in his ear put a grin on his face and a glint in his eye, since killing vermin was his raison d'etre. David and I enjoyed killing rats, but Rusty positively lived for it.

The rats had a system of tunneling that we believed was intricate. The three of us searched for the entrances to the rat tunnels. Rusty found one first, as usual, because his sniffing abilities were better. He put his nose right next to the ground and snuffled and growled all around the yard, tail wagging like a brisk metronome, until he found one of the holes. He looked at us a second, then at the hole, back at us, and then again at the hole, as if to say, "Get on over here now! This is it. Don't lose the spot." All over the yard, he continued to push up dirt with his nose. When he found the other hole, he slammed on the brakes, turned, and expressed with a glance that we were inept helpers, that we should be by his side doing our part. David turned on the outdoor faucet full blast, and hauled the business end of the garden hose to the first hole where I was waiting, and shoved it down into "Rat Central" while Rusty stationed himself at the other hole. With the water on full blast, we fed the hose into the rat hole until it got stuck on a turn in the tunnel.

Rusty stood with all four legs splayed apart, a look of heated anticipation on his face. He did a stiff-jointed prance, cocking his head to the left, right, left. Each time he heard or smelled a rat in the tunnel he feigned an attack, lunging forward with his rear quarters shimmying, then quickly bouncing back to that stiff-legged stance. Tiny, uncontrolled yelps escaping his throat in excitement, his tongue hung out of his face, and his ears straightened out like airplane wings.

When the water had gushed through every living room and hallway of those subterranean condos and the rats started catapulting out of the hole, Rusty became a master of precision. Those critters came so fast and furiously it appeared they were attached nose to tail. They shot out of the hole, bing-bing-bing, rapid-fire.

Rusty put his head close to the hole, grabbed each fleeing rat by the back of the head and gave it a single tremendous shake, snapping its neck. Then he flung it onto an ever-increasing pile a few feet away. Never breaking rhythm or speed, he captured every one of the rats, while we stood by watching, our jaws sagging in adoration and respect.

Eventually, the water bubbled out of the hole where Rusty stood with his pile of prey. When Rusty retired to the shade of the grape arbor, we filled a pan of water for him and discussed the stupidity of rats who would build only two entrances to their tunnels with a guy like Rusty around. David's dad disposed of the carcasses while we drank cold water out of the end of the hose, never thinking twice about where it had been.

Packages Home

MY MOTHER HAD A SPECIAL PLACE where she kept the goods she was saving to send back to the "old country." One day every couple of months, the coffee, sugar, flour, safety pins and sewing needles, shoestrings and clothing she had accumulated to fit a certain box were stacked on the kitchen table, ready for packing. I handed her each item, one at a time, which she placed in the most appropriate position for efficient packing. Then the stories began.

Germany, before the First World War, was the Germany of her childhood. Her father had a stroke in his thirties and could not work thereafter. The family was very poor but never went hungry, due to her mother's resourcefulness. When she spoke of how she and her seven brothers and sisters waited with great expectancy for the bus to bring their mother home from the city, I had great expectancy too. But when she finished the story by saying, "It vas such a joy vhen she brought us a bar of chocolate or an Apfelsine, an orange to share," I felt a hollow ache behind my heart. How could *eight* children find delight in such small portions?

"That's vhy ve use things more than once, mein Susie, and

ve save everything. I hope and pray those days of 'nothing' never come again. But this vorld has verrückte rules. It could happen."

I loved the sound of the names of her family: Emil, Richard, Erna, Gustel, Liesje, Karl and Gerhard, her father, Der Karl, and her mother, Die Ida Oma (Grandmother Ida, pronounced "Dee Eeda Ooma"). She told the stories of childhood mischief set in different parts of her hometown of Kirschweiler, in the hill country between the Moselle and Rhine River valleys of western Germany, near Luxembourg and France.

The shenanigans occurred "über Vollsbach" (over the fields of Vogelsbach), "am Wasserschied" (at the Wasserchied Forest) or "klettern auf die Festung" (climbing to the fortress). I loved the way the German words played with my tongue when I repeated them.

"Ach, one day you have to meet that 'Fratze Gesicht,'* Liesje (pronounced Lees-ya). She's such a Hambelman!"†

The pictures of her in the family photograph album showed a young woman with the thickest of dark braids and a humorous spark shining right out of her. I used to sit with that book in my lap, open its wine-colored cover, and turn the black pages, asking over and over again for the names of every person in every picture and the stories associated with them.

"Ach! That one!" She always smiled when I pointed to

---

* "Fratze Gesicht" colloquially resembles our "funny face."
† A 'Hambelman' is something akin to our Appalachian toy, the Limberjack. It's what my mother called me when I would get into a mood and spontaneously hop and dance around the house.

THROUGH A RUBY WINDOW   71

Liesje. "She vas so full of fun. She vas alvays upside-down or hupsing* and somersaulting in the air. Vhat's the vord for that, Susie?"

"Liesje was a gymnast, Mama," I'd heard this part a hundred times.

"Ja! A gymnast.

"Vhen Liesje grew up," my mother said, "she married Friedrich, and they had four children. They vere very far from Kirschweiler, somevhere in Hesse vhen they got vord that things vere getting more dangerous by the minute and they should head home. And so, Liesje, her husband and children started valking. They vanted to reach Kirschweiler before things got too bad."

She shook the box to make sure everything was snugly packed, then sent me for the twine and scissors. At the table, she used the bread knife to cut the side out of another cardboard box and placed it over the top of the treasures. I stuck my forefingers in the ends of the ball of twine, holding steady as if I were a dispenser. She pulled and wrapped and tied the twine, knotting it at every intersection of twine until each side was divided into sixteen even squares with knots at the nine center intersections.

She moved the box onto a chair and put a large piece of white percale sheet on the table. She set the box down in the middle and wrapped the sheet around it in the manner of Christmas wrapping.

"Liesje and her family vere living on the Lahn River in

---

* my mother's word for springing or leaping

1944. The second vorld var vas undervay and everyone vas frightened and didn't know really vhat vas happening.

"The French and Americans vere advancing vhen the air strikes began. So she and Friedrich took their four children into the forest to hide. The youngest vas just nine months old then. They stayed there vith some other families for a few days in a large hole in the ground that vas covered over vith pine trees. That vay they vere safe and after the American soldiers had passed through, they came out. Tings vere changing rapidly and many people vere being arrested, I don't know vhy.

"So they packed vhat they could carry into a small hand vagon. Everything else, they stored in a neighbor's cellar. The two older children valked, the babies rode in the vagon along vith all the tings they took vith them. They vere not the only ones. There vas a parade of people on the roads, but no one vas happy."

My mother stopped her story for a moment so I could hold the overlaps of the sheet lengthwise across the bottom of the box. With needle and thread she sewed small even stitches, securing the package in the sheet (which was the postal regulation at the time). Her stitching measured out a rhythm, and she began again.

"The armies had set up checkpoints vhere all the people who vere traveling had to stop. Some people vere allowed to pass and others vere sent back for some reason. Liesje and her family met some Polish soldiers in a field who made them stop vith their guns and asked vhere they vere going. They told them they vere going to stay vith friends. But, you know, those soldiers didn't believe anyone. So they valked vith them and followed them right into the house. They saw that Liesje vas telling the truth and finally vent on their vay.

"They valked ten to twenty kilometers a day. (That's between six and twelve miles, like to Edgartown and back.) One evening they came to a small town and, as usual, needed to find a place to spend the night. They stopped at a guest house to ask if there vas room. The owners said they only had room in the barn. Four Russian travelers vere also staying there. Vhen they heard Liesje vas there vith so many children, they insisted she stay in the guest house, and they slept in the barn themselves. So you see, mein Susie, the vorld is filled vith good people."

I thought of how scared I had been the times we had run away, my mother and I, to New York City to get away from my father's drunkenness, and I felt that familiar cold knot in my belly when she talked of the children not knowing where they would sleep at night.

I looked at the package. She was such a meticulous seamstress that the finished seam resembled the twisted cord underneath, the fabric bunching just the slightest between stitches to produce a ridge.

She folded the end fabric into a triangle and I held it to the side as she sewed. The stitching at the point of the triangle always met the ridge of thread from the bottom seam … perfection.

"Each night vhen they came to a town they looked for the

mayor to tell him they vere travelers. He vas bound by law to help strangers passing through his town. Ration cards, vhich acted like money, vere issued so that they could shop and fill their vagon vith vhat they needed for the next day's journey. They kept a little food each day just in case they came to a village vhere nothing could be found.

"One day, at a checkpoint, they received vord that Friedrich had to go. He took the train, and Liesje and the children valked on.

"They passed near Kassel, vhich vas a beautiful city then. Later in the var it vas bombed so heavily that the city had to be rebuilt."

She stopped and went into the living room and came back with a map of Germany. The kitchen table was cluttered with the packing. So we got on the floor and she spread out the map to show me Kassel, then Colbe and Marburg.

"They headed vest then, because they needed to cross the Rhine River to get back to my mother's house, Die Ida Oma."

She pointed to Gladenbach, Herborn, Rennerod, Freiling and Selters, showing me the route they walked, trying to get home to my grandmother.

"This vas the hardest part for them because Liesje had the children by herself then. They vere all travel-vorn and had valked so far that the children, Sigrid, Ute, Uwe, and Hennes, had valked right through the bottoms of their shoes.

"The poor little things, ach! I hate to think how scared they must have been." She looked at me funny and then grabbed me up in her arms the way she did sometimes and nearly yelled, "Ach, how I love you, my Susie-Q!"

"I love you too, Mama," I said, and the cold place I felt for my cousins warmed a little.

She put me down and pointed back to the map. "Here," she said. "They vent to Ransbach and then Baumbach and then finally to your Tante* Gustel's house in Hilgert, over here, near Koblenz." She moved her finger along and let it rest on the city where the Rhine and Moselle rivers flow together.

"At Tante Gustel's, they discovered there vas no vay to get home, because by that time one side of the Rhine vas controlled by the French and the other side by the Americans."

My guts wrenched when I heard that "no vay to get home." I was so afraid this story would make me cry, so I slammed my lips together to press the tears in.

"So," she continued, "they spent the next fifteen years near Gustel."

She refolded the map and tucked it over the refrigerator under the cabinet and we went back to packing.

Her last task was writing the addresses. She used a blue pen and went over and over the letters to make it clear and dark. I spelled it all out loud each time she added a letter. When the address was complete, we stood back and looked at this work of art that would bring necessities and love from their sister and daughter in America.

* * * * * * *

Years later, Liesje made a trip to America to see us. The first night that she and my mother were together in our house,

---

* Aunt

I couldn't sleep because the two of them were sitting cross-legged on my mother's bed in their flannel pajamas making a ruckus.

Like schoolgirls, they were wound up to bursting with the joy of one another's company. With no need to get up the next morning, reminiscences spilled out and piled up on one another, withstanding one sisterly interruption after another. They laughed so loud and hard that I couldn't sleep.

Their delight was so contagious, I laughed out loud myself. I finally got up and went in to tell them they were in danger of waking the dead. An audience only encouraged them. They laughed and cried and my mother tried to translate. But she was so excited that she spoke to Liesje in English, translating it into German for me.

When they started to talk about the packages sent home, I paid very close attention. This, after all, was my story as well. Liesje talked about the contents and how they rejoiced in those simple things arriving from Jettche. She talked about the prom dress that my mother had sent from a neighbor that arrived just in time for a wedding. The bride had not been able to get anything special for there was nothing to be had, but there it was, adding another layer of joy to her day.

Liesje talked about that long journey across Germany that ended at Gustel's house in Hilgert. It was close to that time that my mother had been to a rummage sale at the Stone Church in Vineyard Haven, and found something that she thought would be good for the next package.

Watching the two sisters tell this story together, each

speaking on top of the other's words so that it was sometimes a curious monologue with two voices, sometimes a dialog, I waited for the end of the story I loved so much.

My mother had the floor: "I found them at the sale, all in a row. I thought, 'Ach! Somebody over there can surely use these.' So I bought them all for ten cents a pair."

"And vhen ve arrived at Gustel's," Liesje finished, "barefoot and tired and so happy to see family, there came a package from Jettche. Inside vith the coffee and sugar and other things that vere so velcome, there vere four pairs of little shoes that perfectly fit four very bare little pairs of feet."

The look that passed between those two sisters then held a cord of memory that bound them, its pain and joy resonating, entwining the two again and again. That forty-cent gift between sisters was a tangible symbol of the resourcefulness that their mother passed on to them, deep and strong and indestructible.

The silence in the room was thick. "Ach du lieber, Jettche, es ist schon fünf uhr."* Liesje leapt off the bed and ran to the corner of the room. Running back to the foot of her bed, she sprang straight up and somersaulted in the air before she landed in bed and yanked the covers to her chin.

My mother said, "See that Hambelman? Didn't I tell you?"

---

* "Oh my dear, Jettche, it's already five o'clock."

On the Wing

WHEN DAVID AND I PLAYED "Jackknife," he always won, I always lost. It was his jackknife, so he made the rules, though not necessarily before he took his turn.

We considered this game to be very serious business. Facing each other, we knelt in the grass, our eyes locked in a trancelike gaze.

Rusty sat to my right, David's left. As our dedicated spectator, he intently watched the path of the knife from the time it left a hand until it stuck in the ground. He had that curious look that dogs get when they view human activity with disdain. He knew this game was trouble long before we did, and said so with many stiff tilts of the head and looks of consternation.

David said, "OK, let's do the big one now." So he balanced the knife point and flipped his wrist. In three graceful loops, the knife arced over his head and stuck in the lawn three feet behind him. He said it was three feet, though as usual he didn't use a measuring device.

"OK, Klein, your turn."

I looked straight into David's eyes, balanced the point of

the open jackknife on the middle finger of my left hand, brought my right palm down hard on the inside of my left elbow, and flipped the knife up into the air. He had flipped the knife over his head. Whether or not I could repeat that, matching the distance it landed from us and the number of revolutions it made in the air, determined the winner. By the worried look that hung on his face I could see that I had perfectly executed the toss and that I would win for the first time. His eyes were watching the twirling of the knife, though they were supposed to be staring into my eyes. I then noticed from the corner of my eye that Rusty also had a worried look on his face.

The dog's eyes and David's were both tracing the path of the knife. I was captivated by their captivation, when all of a sudden, "THUNK," the knife came down smack on the crown of my skull. By grace, it landed butt end first, then fell to the ground with a soft thud.

I saw Rusty shudder as I rubbed my head. David's eyes rolled in his head. He said, "Phhhhhhew! This knife business is too dangerous. Let's get the gun."

So we packed up the jackknife and went inside to get the BB gun David had gotten for Christmas. Wagging my finger in his face, I chided, "Your father said, 'Never, never, never, never, never, never, never, never, NEVER use the gun when no one's home.'"

He pointedly said, "No one's home. So who's gonna know?" which meant I was sworn to secrecy. "I'm gonna take my turn first, then you can have it for awhile," which meant I might get a turn by next Tuesday.

The truth was, though, that David, even at seven years old, was a deadeye, just like his dad, "One-shot Nella," who had taught him. I said, "So what're we gonna shoot?" figuring that we would line up the Welch's grape juice cans on the barbecue again.

He said, "Well, we haven't had lunch yet."

I said, "Yeah, but El said she'd come back and make us some later."

"Well, then, let's get her something to cook," he said, scanning the yard. "Look up there!"

I followed his gaze and said, "They're kinda small," as Rusty covered his eyes with his paws.

"We'll get lots," he said as he aimed the gun at the chokecherry tree and brought down the first starling. They all flew up and around and settled down again after much chirping and fluttering of wings.

We both looked at Rusty, expecting him to go get the bird. He *was* a retriever, for crying out loud. This was his birthright. But the dog just looked from us to the dead bird and back again, with a look of disbelief on his face. Rusty did ducks and geese. Apparently the retrieval of starlings was beneath his dignity, because he didn't budge.

So *I* had to be the retriever. I picked it up by its skinny little legs and brought it back to begin the pile of what would amount to a dozen sparrows and starlings, while the dog looked on in disgust. David used fourteen BBs for twelve birds.

We brought them into the house to clean. Over the years,

we'd seen a veritable parade of quail, woodcock, pheasant, ducks and geese come through the back door, so we knew enough about pluckin' and guttin' to take care of the day's yield. There was always something hanging upside down off the end of the clothesline pole with its tongue hanging out, waiting to become dinner. So we were quite used to the process by which animals became food.

We stood near the sink, which reached right up underneath my chin, and lined up the birds on the cutting board, heads toward the window. David, who had recently proven he was better with a knife, chose the biggest one he could find. One whack of that huge blade and a dozen heads rolled off the board. Next, twenty-four feet were chopped and pushed away with the blade of the knife.

Plucking was a tedious affair. If you're plucking a goose, there's plenty to grip by the handful. But these fowl were so tiny that it was a fingertip deal. The feathers were so lightweight that they fluttered up and filled the kitchen air. It took a long while of teeny fingers full of pluck, pluck, plucking, before we got the job done as effectively as could be expected under the circumstances. Then we gutted each one with a single motion of the forefinger.

Because we were curious, we opened up all the stomach sacks to see what the birds had been eating. As we smeared the contents across the Formica we made a lot of scientific comparisons; as many as we could, of course, with no control group. We discovered they had mostly eaten a variety of seeds, which had been our pre-experimental prediction.

We then soaked the birds in salted water like El always did to diminish the gamy flavor, while we set the table and discussed a recipe. We didn't know much about culinary measurements, so we figured a stick of butter would do. Out came the biggest cast-iron frying pan. We cranked the burner up to high and tossed in the butter. We found it doesn't take very long for an electric burner set on high to melt butter, turn it a really pretty shade of brown, and send great curls of smoke up to cling to the ceiling.

We tossed those little carcasses one at a time into that sea of butter. Because they'd been soaking in salt water and we hadn't dried them off, they made explosive sizzling sounds when they hit the grease. We thought the spatter effect quite an artful design. We turned the birds as they browned on one side and then another.

Everything was looking mighty fine and lunch was nearly ready when we heard the back door slam.

We turned to see Nelson framed by the door casing. The sizzling of the birds was suddenly a terrifically sharp sound in the otherwise silent kitchen.

Our eyes met his, and a look I could not name passed over his face. After what seemed a very long time, he shook his head, turned around and walked out the door.

We looked at one another, each wearing a dark grimace of fear and anticipation. But he didn't return. We knew we were going to get it this time.

David said, "I think we better eat these birds while we still can." So we dished out the birds and sat down to nibble little sparrow drumsticks and pile up little white starling bones in teeny-tiny heaps. They tasted just like chicken, only sweeter. Ah, there's nothing like bagging it and eating it in the same day.

We cleaned up as best we could, and summoning great courage, went outside to see what Nelson was up to. We waited, but he never said a word. So neither did we; at least, not until after Thanksgiving dinner of 1988 when David and I got to reminiscing about that long-ago feast we had prepared.

With tongue in cheek I asked Nelson, "Do you remember the time you happened in on David and me cooking up all those sparrows and starlings in the frying pan?"

He said, "Yup."

"Well, we've been waiting for that punishment an awfully long time now. You want to tell us why you just left us there like that and never said a word?"

He leaned back in his recliner, and with a grin and a twinkle he said, "Well, I could smell something delicious cooking when I got out of the Jeep. So I went in to see what was going on. It wasn't what I expected. The kitchen was a wreck. There were feathers everywhere, bird guts smeared on the counter and cabinet doors, grease clinging to every surface of my new paint job, little bird heads and feet all over the place, and the two of you grinning like fools.

"I was about to start yelling about using that gun when I wasn't home, when I suddenly recalled that some years back, my own father had walked in the back door of our house and found a scene exactly like that. It was all I could do to get out to the backyard as quickly as I could and laugh and laugh."

It took me thirty years to figure out why David was who he was. Some things are just plain genetic.

Negotiating the Narrows

EARLY EVERY DAY DURING LENT, through the branches of the maple tree outside my bedroom window, I watched the old Portuguese women bending over their rosaries, their short mantillas fluttering as they hurried to morning mass at Sacred Heart Church. The little church sufficed for the small year-round congregation and saved on winter heating bills, while in summer, the big church downtown accommodated the addition of vacationers to the flock.

I didn't know much about Catholicism, but I was certainly intrigued by the accouterments. In their homes, the old women were never far away from their rosary beads, which they often kept in their apron pockets, wrapped in the rare finery of a white lace handkerchief. I sometimes came upon one of them fingering the beads and mumbling the "Hail Mary" as I popped through someone's back door. If a family experienced rough times, I could always tell because the old one would be incommunicado even though in our presence, going about her chores as if entranced, fingering and mumbling, present but not available. I was fascinated by those beads, but I could not understand why, when those old women had something so beautiful, they did not wear them around their necks. Passing a bedroom door left ajar, I caught a glimpse of an even more ornate string of rosary beads on top of a bureau or nightstand, draped across a picture of the Sacred Heart of Jesus, which I thought beautiful and frightening at the same time. Until I happened in on Ma Phillips's front parlor for the first time, I was unaware that there could be anything more beautiful than the beads.

Front parlors in a house like Ma's were simply arranged and reserved for visitors on special occasions, so the interior door was always closed. Thick lace curtains made it impossible to see through the windows. Her outside door on the porch had an opaque frosted design on the beveled oval window, so I had never seen that room. One day when her arthritis was acting up, she asked me to help her carry a bunch of newly-crocheted antimacassars into the parlor, though she called them doilies. I was always eager to explore something new. So it was from behind her wide skirt that I saw that one full corner of the parlor had been transformed into a bright miracle.

Beginning in the corner at my eye level, rounded shelves decreased in size as they ascended to the ceiling like a wedding cake. Each level was covered with a wine-red cloth with a white Portuguese lace overlay matching the curtains that were pulled back about halfway up from the floor and pinned to the wall on either side. The lace on the bottom shelf cascaded to the floor in undulating curves. On each landing candles burned in small red glasses, their flames illuminating the faces of at least a dozen dolls ranging in size from those that could fit in a hand to a few over a foot tall. Reflections of candlelight flickering on their faces suggested that they were capable of changing expression.

When I asked to play with the big one, Ma explained that they could not be handled or played with, though she let me hold the one I pointed to so I could see how finely it was made. He had the sweetest face I had ever seen, was dressed in lace and velvet, and wore a gold crown on his nearly shoulder-length porcelain hair. She said that this was an altar and that the "dolls" were saints and so they were very special because they could hear her when she needed to talk to God. I was mesmerized! The whole corner was a fantasy and its sacredness was apparent. I was intrigued by the idea of dolls I couldn't play with and candles burning in an empty room.

Fire was dominating our lives at that time because the neighborhood men, most of whom were volunteer firemen, were battling a huge blaze in the woods behind our house. The sea winds fed the fire, making it last an eternity. The women were a blur of flowered aprons rushing past with sandwiches, casseroles, muffins, and cakes which they loaded into Jeeps and trucks and took to the woods for the men. As the blaze threatened to consume more and more acres, the men came home in shifts, mixing their pungent odors of wood smoke, sweat, and fear with the comfortable smell of strong coffee brewing nonstop in urns borrowed from church halls. Restored by a bath and sleep, my father headed back to the fire with the other men who had also taken a break, and the women kept on cooking.

And here was Ma Phillips burning candles unattended in the parlor while she worked in the kitchen. It became a day of wonder: beautiful dolls I couldn't play with in ornate display in the simplest of homes, and unattended flames in the face of the largest forest fire the island had ever witnessed. My expanding world was increasingly more curious.

My friend Debbie Viera had rosary beads that she let me look at sometimes, but not for very long. They, like Ma Phillips's alluring saints, were clearly not playthings.

When we got a little older, we frequently stayed overnight on Friday at each other's house. We'd have all of Saturday to watch cartoons and play. I loved going there, not only to play with Debbie, but because she had a lilac bedroom (no one that I knew had a purple room in the 1950s) and her mother never referred to us as children or kids. She would say, "Would you folks come in now? It's time for lunch." It made us feel so grown up.

We often had so much fun that we would ask to spend another night together, but the answer was always a definitive "no." It took ages for me to understand that an overnight stay on a Saturday night brought up the *church* question, and I guess it seemed easier for the adults to avoid it. Debbie was a Catholic and I was a Methodist. That there was any difference beyond the possession of rosary beads and Ma Phillips's altar was unknown to me. I thought there were many houses of God only because the whole town couldn't fit into one all at the same time.

Surprisingly, and to our great delight, when we were

seven, I was allowed to spend my first Saturday night at Debbie's. I packed my church clothes along with my pajamas into the zippered belly of a fluffy yellow-orange tiger bag someone had given me. It was a way of leaving the security of home while having your suitcase double as a fuzzy friend for cuddling. We giggled into the night, stuffing our heads under the pillows to keep from waking the house.

The next morning we were excited because summer was upon us, and we knew that meant we would be going to the big church together. As soon as I stepped into church, however, it became evident that what I knew about Catholicism was inadequate for the task ahead. My reaction could not have been more intense had I entered the Vatican or Germany's Wiesekirche, the Queen of Rococo. If the Trinity Methodist Church I attended in the Campgrounds wore a quaint little tweed suit and sensible shoes, Our Lady Star of the Sea sparkled in a sequined ball gown and spike heels.

My black patent leather shoes branded me a Methodist as soon as the first beam of light bounced off the uppers and made searchlight sweeps across the vaulted ceiling. But I was so dumb founded by the beauty of the sunlight streaming through the stained glass that I forgot about my shoes.

Debbie and I were allowed to sit by ourselves. Walking ahead of me, she chose a forward pew on the left side. Gawking at the decor, I barely caught sight of her genuflection and crossing. For the life of me, I couldn't figure out what she had done. Filled with the sudden panic of someone who has blundered into a secret society and wishes to remain unnoticed,

I took a shot at it. Bent at the knees, I made some motions with my hands that probably meant something closer to "Throw a curve ball left of the plate" than "In the name of the Father, the Son, and the Holy Ghost."

Star of the Sea had a three-and-a-half inch vertical wooden runner on the floor that strung the pews together, which I had neglected to notice as I pondered genuflection. The sound of my patent leather toes' impact on the runner ricocheted back and forth against the colored glass as I took a flailing header face first across the kneelers. That did it for Debbie and me. We split our sides laughing all through the mass (which I mistakenly called a service), as I tried to keep up with the rhythm of stand up, sit down, kneel, kneel, kneel.

Could it be that the murmurs we heard buzzing through the church were actually, "Fee Fie Fo Fist, we smell the blood of a Methodist!"? We were still gasping for air through our muffled laughter when the incense bearer arrived. The priest, waving that huge ball and chain all over the place, met our eyes with a pointed glare as he whooshed by, dispensing an asphyxiating fog which knocked us both into silence.

The alluring drone of the Latin and the immense drama of the mass were totally unlike my Sunday morning experiences. I was used to participating in the action as opposed to witnessing it, and I truly missed having the chance to sing. I comprehended nothing but was most certainly fascinated, and couldn't wait for the following Sunday to bring Debbie to my church. Then we'd really have something to talk about!

All week long, I kept inviting her to Trinity, but she would not respond. Finally, I asked her what was wrong. "I can stay over Saturday night," she said seriously, "but my mom will pick me up for church in the morning." When I asked why she couldn't just come with me to church, she said, "I can't. It's a sin for a Catholic to go to another church. God will strike me dead."

I laughed at her seriousness and said, "No, He won't! I went to *your* church and *I'm* still alive!"

"But you're not a Catholic!" she said. I could see that she felt sorry for me, which I thought a waste of pity, as I couldn't see that one or the other was better, only different, and it was the difference that I found exciting. No matter what I said, she wouldn't budge; nor could she because it would be sinning. This whole high drama of the hierarchy of sin was new to me. As I understood Methodism, if you got involved in anything short of breaking a Commandment, you were simply on your own to turn it around and try not to repeat the infringement. It took every waking moment and some of my sleeping ones as well before I finally figured it out.

I knew from Sunday School that Moses was an *old* man when he had his experience on the mount. I reckoned he must have been deaf in one ear, catching only half of what God had said or else hearing it in a "creative" way, as the elderly are wont to do. The only explanation I could come up with was that there might be two Gods, one a little stricter than the other, and Moses, due to his auditory deficiency, didn't catch it. But that didn't stop the confusion for me as "Thou shalt not have other *gods* before me" gave me to believe that perhaps there might be *many*, and they were all duking it out for first position in the eyes of humankind. Trying to discern which might be the top God made for long days in my secret place in a small pine grove in the forest behind Wing Road, where I held lengthy discussions with a pantheon of deities in an effort to get some perspective. I found great relief when it suddenly occurred to me that I could save myself a goodly amount of anguish if I checked in with the dozen or so authorities we had living right next door.

I tiptoed across the driveway, climbed up onto Ma Phillips's porch and peeked through a gap in the lace curtains into the living room. There, in between the flickering red votive candles, were the beautiful porcelain saints. But instead of the candlelight illuminating those sweet faces, all willy-nilly and at odd angles, two dozen tiny feet were waving above red velvet and white lace hems. The saints were all standing on their heads, clear evidence I wasn't the only one who was confused.

Just then Ma Phillips came into the room. When she caught sight of her beloved altar, she let out a thin shriek, grabbed her handkerchief out of her apron pocket and held it to her mouth in shock, her rosary beads dangling noisily back and forth from her fist. With both hands she reached to right the tallest upended saint, unleashing the string of Portuguese phrases that had backed up behind her handkerchief.

I had never seen her angry before. I fled before she saw me because she might have thought it was I who had turned her holy crew topsy-turvy. I secretly knew that they had done it themselves to show me that the answers would not come easily. Though I would later learn that it was the deed of Ma Phillips's son who played pranks when in his cups, I was certain I had received a heavenly sign.

Over the next few weeks, my confusion and curiosity battled it out over the God issue, and I began to get an inkling that the crux of the problem lay not above, but below. That inkling was spawned by conversations with my Catholic friends about confession. I said Methodists confessed to God as well, though we didn't go to any particular place to do it, because you could talk to God anywhere, anytime. They looked at me as if I was from another planet and said, "You're supposed to confess on Wednesdays to the priest, not to God!" More conflicting information; I knew Ma spoke to God in her living room.

It seemed a grand idea to have an opportunity scheduled weekly (if you needed it) to clean the slate of any wrongdoings. At least, I thought so, until I discovered that not only was the "opportunity" mandatory, which made it a sin *not* to confess your sins, but that my friends were sometimes so well-behaved (and fearful of being struck dead by lightning) that they had to regularly make up ill deeds to confess to the priest. When I said, "But I thought *lying* was a *sin*," they told me (with the circular logic of children) that of course it was, *usually*, but not in this case, because they didn't mean it. They exchanged looks of eye-rolling frustration because I just didn't get it. I said, "Oh! I see!" And I did, for just a moment. But confusion won the battle and formal religion for me had sprung an unstoppable leak which would lead to a lifetime of puzzlement.

It was a curiosity that was fed by wondering just how many *other* people in town (perhaps even those not of the Methodist persuasion) might question all these things. My mother often said, "There's nothing new under the sun," so I knew I couldn't have thought this up all on my own. There was, however, no one I felt I could comfortably ask. So my conversations with God increased in complexity as I grappled with the two inter-pretations available to me. Had I been privy to Zen perhaps, or Hinduism or Thlingit totem worship, I might never have had a mortal conversation again, simply for lack of time.

I continued to go to the Catholic church occasionally after Saturday night pajama parties and such, mostly to marvel at the incredible sculpture and ornamentation, but especially to be with my friends. The cadence of the Latin, so much like song, was a rhythmic invitation to enter a trance, though at the time I would have called it a daydream. But neither church offered me the uplifted feeling that my daydreams under the pines provided.

At Trinity, I marveled at the variety of women's hats and at just how many circles there were in the patterns on the walls and ceilings. I counted the thousands every week with my newly acquired multiplication skills to see if the number had changed. It was the one thing pertaining to religion that remained constant, and for that I was grateful.

*   *   *   *   *   *   *

The July after all the girls in my class (except me) made First Communion, Joe, a friend of the family, came to the house to ask me a favor. My mother called me in from the backyard and said, "The Holy Ghost Feast parade is on Saturday. You know how all the girls who make Communion carry the ends of the ribbons for the pillow. They need one more girl; would you like to be in the parade with your friends?"

I was stunned! It took me a long time to answer because I was having a lengthy conversation with myself. Now here was a dilemma.

The girls encircled the pillow carrier, who was really the one who got the attention, for poised on the pillow was the crown of Mary, the mother of Jesus! This had nothing to do with Methodists. I couldn't believe Joe didn't know the rules. He was Catholic, for God's sake! Didn't he know that if I was helping to carry the crown of the Queen of Heaven that round about the time the parade hit the bottom of Circuit Avenue, a well-directed bolt of lightning would strike the lot of them dead, leaving an entire grade level of Catholic girls in a steaming puddle in the street by the movie theater?

My only image of human death was from watching the wicked witch on "The Wizard of Oz" melt out of a pair of ruby slippers. So I figured that was how it would look if God struck them dead. The thought of being the only living girl left in my class filled me with dread, so I said the first thing to come to mind. "No, I don't have a white lace Communion dress."

"We can borrow one from somebody who made Communion last year," Joe said, blowing my chances of escaping.

My mother said, "Would you like to do it?"

I shook my head furiously.

So Joe went on to some other mother-daughter duo in town with his arts of persuasion. Having single-handedly saved the entire seven-year-old Oak Bluffs female population from celestial annihilation, I headed straight for Ma Phillips's altar to make sure the saints were upright. Then I retreated to the pine grove to have yet another conversation with the beings on high.

To further confuse things, shortly thereafter Debbie was allowed to attend Trinity with me in spite of the threat of being struck dead. The conversation on comparative religions I had anticipated was well worth the wait. She enjoyed not having to kneel, and we both walked away from church that day unharmed and questioning what all the brouhaha was about in the first place.

Years later I would conclude that Joe was trying to find a way to fill a need—an uncontrollable ribbon fluttering from the pillow supporting Mary's crown would not do. In order to offer the respect and adulation due the Queen of Heaven, he chose to bend the rules. But at seven, I was just beginning to fathom the shades of gray, just beginning to understand the elasticity of the rules that the adults made.

* * * * * * *

Over the years that followed, I was making my peace with confusion and thinking I could accept the conflicting interpretations, when two things occurring one after the other completely upended my progress in understanding humankind. So deeply in opposition to Sunday's teachings were these events that I realized the entire scheme of following up the "saying" with the "doing" was completely out of balance.

At recess at the Oak Bluffs School one day, I was playing by myself, because there had been some sort of secret whispered among the others all morning. Because there were only seventeen of us in class, secrets generally had very short lives. I was feeling low because, oddly, I hadn't been let in on the conversation. As I was walking across the playground, one, then another of my friends ran up to me, surely, I thought, to let me in on the secret. But instead of the warmth I expected from an intimate secret, I felt the cold steel wall that accompanies ostracism. One, then another, and another—at least a dozen kids made a circle around me, pointing their fingers at me in unison to a quickening staccato rhythm of their jeers. "Na- zi! Na-zi! Na-zi!" I spun around, looking at their faces, not believing that yesterday we were all friends and today I was clearly despised for something I did not comprehend.

Degradation is a bottomless pit with walls dank and slimy, making it impossible to get a handhold to try to come up for air. I was choking with tears. I had heard the word "Nazi" before, knew it to be a horrible thing, but didn't really know what "Nazi" meant. All I could think was how could this be? How could they all know I am this despicable thing and I not know it about myself? I tried to run. But they held hands, flinging me back into the center of the circle, and when I tried to break them apart, they chanted louder, twisting their pitiless features into a contortion of righteousness. I finally ran, making as if to race through a pair of clasped hands. I could see as I got closer that they held tighter and braced themselves, since they knew I was trying to break out of the cage they had made. Just as I reached them, I ducked and slipped under a pair of rigid arms and fled. Tears streamed for over an hour and invisibly for weeks. Feeling unaccepted and disqualified from a group I loved and thought loved me was a cruel lesson that left me empty and very shaky.

It was my friend Ernie Garvin who put his arm around me and walked me home after school that day. He said it would be okay, they'd forget about it. I said *they* might, but that *I* never would.

When my mother came home from work that evening, she could see something was wrong. I didn't want to tell her. She pressed. I asked only one question. "Are we Nazis?"

Whatever went through her mind at that moment created a visible spark as she flew into a rage, half English, half German, all of it completely incomprehensible. But I got the point. She clearly meant "no." I was so relieved that I started crying all over again. She ended her bilingual tirade by forbidding me to ever utter the hideous word in the house again. I accepted the edict from She Who Knows All, but still didn't know what a Nazi really was. So I headed downtown to the one place I thought I might find some answers, the Oak Bluffs Library, that magnificent repository of information, offering balm and clarity for those who have parents who lean towards censorship.

When I found "Nazi" in the encyclopedia and then read a magazine story, I was completely horrified by the savage details and by my friends' willingness to associate me with such base barbarity.

I told my friend Ernie about my research the next day at school. He said he had known but couldn't tell me the day it happened because he couldn't bear to explain. We talked about the strangeness of the incident. Our vocabularies did not yet contain the word "irony," but we had just experienced it. In naming me the villain, our schoolmates became villainous. We were intrigued by the paradox, and it somehow lessened the pain. After that, our friendship blossomed, and we often met halfway to school where our paths crossed at the edge of the field on Franklin Street.

*   *   *   *   *   *   *

The second incident that tested my faith in human nature occurred a few weeks after the Nazi episode. Things had smoothed over with the fluctuating loyalties characteristic of children, and I was delighted to be part of the group again. I had not yet learned how small our community was, nor how watchful some of its members. The cold truth came when a friend of the family quietly took me aside one day and said that she thought it best if I wasn't so friendly with Ernie. No one had ever said anything like that before, so I was confused. "Why not?" I asked.

In a caring and solicitous way, she said, "It'd be better for you if you'd stick to your own kind."

I thought, "Damn! Here's that religion thing again!"

"But Ernie and I go to Sunday School together. He's a Methodist!"

Through not-quite-clenched teeth, she whispered, "I don't mean he's not a Methodist. I mean he's not white." Her demeanor was of one who wishes to protect.

The wound in my gut from a few weeks before was still raw. The reaction I had to this woman's statement ignited the realization that social injustice would be a recurring theme that would keep that wound from healing for a lifetime.

Beyond her gaze I struggled with nausea. There were just too many feelings to handle all at once. The Catholic/Methodist issue paled in comparison to this one, though I saw they were related. I thought I'd continue to make myself smaller and smaller and finally when I just blinked out like a firefly, the pain would stop. But I hadn't allowed for the warrior factor. That retreating heart did an about-face, filling and pulsing, growing until it burst out of its confines, pain and all.

The teachings of Sunday School were hanging like holiday banners in front of my field of vision. "Love Your Neighbor ... *except when* ...." "God Is Love ... *but only if* ...." "We Are All Sisters and Brothers ... *unless, of course* ...." In a few weeks' time, these had all turned to ashes in the insidious fires of bigotry.

I had seen bigotry before but I didn't know it had a name. People sometimes talked about the Inkwell, the bathing beach in town where the summer "coloreds" swam. But I did not *discover* bigotry until I felt its knife point personally. What had happened to my mother's teaching? "There's good and bad in every batch. It's the vay of the vorld. You've got to take one person at a time." Suddenly, a flash of clarity completely overwhelmed me. I was not a Nazi, but I was a German. Not one's actions, but one's cultural identity incited bigotry. A veil fluttered to the floor and I saw clearly that if I was branded as a Nazi, then I was also a Nigger, a Wop, a Spic, a Jap, a Kyke. In our differences lay our similarity. It didn't matter what the brand name was, just so long as there *was* a brand, a single brand with enough spellings to identify whomever was different, whomever might be put down and kept down.

My trips to the library proved to me that this game of social hierarchy was neither an island phenomenon, nor purely an American phenomenon, but rather a strange corruption of the human spirit, a spirit so in need of its own affirmation that over and over again people take the easy way out, pointing the finger at the "other" and naming it evil. The finger pointing is so much easier than confronting the difficult internal work of naming one's own shadow spirit.

I had learned that self-worth could be bought at the high price of bigotry, and it was a price I was unwilling to pay. From my Sunday school teachings I understood that religion intended to set forth a positive model of behavior, but the leak that had sprung in religion had become a torrent, and I never did succeed in making sense of the whole of it.

* * * * * * *

Though I might still have been able to look to my religion for understanding, another incident got in my way. It was a Sunday sermon soon after focused on original sin, and in no uncertain terms, womankind got pinned with the blame.

That did it! The proverbial straw had just been tossed upon the camel's back. I felt I had been smacked square in the pelvis with a Bible. Did I really see the collective woman assembled there drop her shoulders, hang her head, and let her power dissipate into the patriarchal air? It was all I could do not to stand up in church and take a show of hands to see if I was the only one who refused to buy that ideological corset designed by the emperor's tailors. Was there no one else present who felt as supremely uncomfortable as I (how about just a little uncomfortable) with this idea? Could that be what originally ignited the burning bush, a woman's thoughts of balancing accounts?

Female responsibility for the original sin brought with it the condemnation of all women for all time. I found the very idea so completely absurd that I left the church that day and never returned. I sometimes return to churches to marvel at the architecture, but never do I return to church.

I went that afternoon to my secret spot in the woods to sort out my impressions of a world that had become frighteningly contradictory. Lying on a spongy bed of pine needles, I watched small lamb-like clouds moving east across bright patches of sky above the uppermost branches. The movement gave me that curious "illusion" of the earth moving and sky standing still.

As I stared up through the delicate white pines, a soft breeze whispered a numinous song—no interpretations, no biases, no exclusions, but rather a song of all that is seen and unseen, affirming the one indelible Truth I had learned in Sunday School: God is Everywhere. In that moment, and forever, the grove of pines became my private cathedral.

* * * * * * *

As with all things, we weave experiences into the fabric of our lives, and we go on. I learned to do the "small community dance," to shake down my own experiences into manageable little packages in a warehouse of memories to keep a perspective on the community as a whole, which I adore, without forgetting its imperfections, which include my imperfections. "Forgive and forget," the church and my mama said; admirable advice, but perhaps irresponsible. Forgetting means leaving the responsibility to change things to someone else.

Oak Bluffs has been a summer resort for hundreds of years, and specifically for African-Americans since the early part of the century. I have always found the labeling of a section of beach "The Inkwell" a supreme embarrassment. As a child I was naive enough to think that only the white people knew that the whites called it that. Clearly word has leaked out, for thirty-five years later (who would have thought?) this beautiful stretch of beach has become an exclusive, sought-after place to visit. And as with other "in" spots, people tend to let others know they have been there. All over town now, people are sporting white T-shirts with black stick figures on the back and "The Inkwell" in big letters across the front—testimony that at least one piece of racism has been turned smack on its head. Maybe they have forgiven, maybe not; no one has forgotten. I smile a little smile, watching the world change, however slowly.

Our neighborhood has changed as well. Ma Phillips's house has been bought and sold a number of times since her death. I don't know where her beautiful saints have ended up. My guess is that each time the status quo is challenged, each time an unacceptable precept gets shaken up until its bottom finally falls out, one of those saints, wherever it might be, is awakened by the reverberation, plants its feet flat, and stands tall.

Trafficking in Mischief

MY MOTHER WORKED a split shift as cook at the hospital, so I ate dinner six evenings each week with the Amarals. For David and me, the dishes argument was one of our daily rituals. But we usually found some amusement to settle it, whether towel-whipping, spraying each other with the rinse hose, or our very favorite ....

This was the mischief that caused both Eleanor and Nelson to threaten slamming us "into the middle of next week," as they put it. We secured the sink drain, poured in as much liquid detergent as we thought we could get away with, and got that water to thundering. Nelson's a plumber, so they always had fabulous water pressure. In seconds we had four inches of water and a monolith of suds nearly as tall as me rising out of the sink.

We got the form pan (now called a Bundt pan), the one that makes a circular cake with a hole in the middle. We held it high over our heads and slammed that form pan as hard as we could into the sink, shooting the suds up through the central funnel as if through a cannon. We repeated that over and over until we had an array of dripping frothy stalactites hanging from the ceiling.

Eleanor was only ten feet away in the living room, and by the tone of her voice, she had had enough of our shenanigans. "Knock it off, you two! Why don't you kids go play in the traffic?" El and Nel didn't have to worry because *they* knew that *we* knew that that was *not* a *literal* directive. We knew her intent was only to terminate the annoying behavior we were enjoying.

But that night we were in a literal mood. A raised-eyebrow look of conspiracy passed between us. We said not a word, dropped our dishwashing paraphernalia, and headed for the cellar, the psychic communication so strong between us that the air was shimmering.

We took what we needed from the cellar, tied the wire from the maple trees in David's yard to the oak tree across the street on the corner of Franklin Avenue, twisted it securely, and snipped it with a pair of cutting pliers. Then we crawled under the bushes and waited to see what would appear out of the low-lying wispy spring fog that was swirling up Wing Road.

We fetched up the fenders of a number of wrathful citizens out there in the dark, and they weren't too pleased. We did pride ourselves in being clever, and we thought this a pretty clever trick. But we soon discovered we would have been far more clever had we strung the wire in front of someone else's house.

Beach Party

BABY LINDA WAS SITTING in her little recliner chair, happy as a clam at high tide, on top of the table, directly between the watermelon and the cardboard box that contained the plastic knives, forks, and spoons, paper towels, Kleenex, garbage bags, diapers, formula, and cooking utensils. Another box on the table had hamburger and hot dog rolls, a bag of marshmallows and those ingenious hinged grills that sandwich hamburgers and hot dogs so they don't fall into the fire.

Coolers with crushed and cubed ice at the bottom were ready for the perishables. Others were packed with waxed cardboard milk containers that had been washed, filled with water, and set in the freezer overnight, making half-gallon blocks of ice. Block ice not only lasted longer than cubes, it also melted slowly through the course of the day, remained in the container, and could be used for drinking.

Mustard, relish, mayonnaise, pickles, chopped onions, ketchup, hot peppers, pickled onions, hamburger, hot dogs, linguica, and summer fruits filled the coolers. A big box of potatoes and onions and a burlap bag full of corn finished out the food list. Cases of beer and soda which would later be iced down in a metal rubbish can were piled on the kitchen table, better known as "Beach Party Prep Central," which afforded us a perfect place to check things off the lists.

My sister Eleanor was and is a person of lists. She had lists, and lists of lists, all executed in a swooping, swirling hand-writing that would have made Palmer beam. With a mind that sees spatial relationships in a twinkling, she knew exactly how much of what would fit most efficiently where. And she just loved crossing off the "what" once it was "where," proving that progress was being made.

My job was pretty much to empty the refrigerator, pack the boxes, and carry them to the Jeep. As I packed and hauled, I talked to the baby, packed some more, tickled the water-melon, tickled the baby, and Eleanor checked some more items off the lists. I had time to hide my library books under the front passenger seat where they would be safe from all the boys. El went down to the cellar to find the wire shellfish bas-kets and yelled, "You got the towels?" I headed for the bathroom closet. A full day beach party is not a "one person, one towel" affair, so I took *all* the towels.

There wasn't room for yet another box in the back of the Jeep, so I flung the snorkels, goggles, and flippers in from the edge of the tailgate, a pair at a time, letting them land where they might. I pushed three huge inflated inner tubes in through the back, completely obscuring Eleanor's rear view. Because she drove as if all the demons of hell were after her anyway, an obstructed rearview mirror was hardly an inconvenience.

When a line was drawn through every item on El's lists except for what we needed to pick up at Pacheco's* on the way, we stuffed the wire baskets between the inner tubes, balanced our six-month-old baby bundle and the watermelon among the paraphernalia, and whistled for the dog. Rusty bounded onto the open tailgate, always willing to bounce along the rough roads at the mercy of the strength of the hinges.

He always did fine back there, his forepaws hanging off the tailgate. Most people thought Rusty panted a lot because it was summer and he had so much blond hair. But I knew he was simply grinning so wide his tongue hung out. There were no tailgate laws then, none that we abided by at any rate, so he was in his favorite place (second only to the cool shade of the grape arbor), safe and secure except for that wicked bump at the top of the hill where Katama and Naushon Avenues meet. There was no stop sign then at the bottom by Waban Park.

El hit that bump at the same speed she would an unencumbered straightaway, causing everything in the Jeep, including Rusty, to hover, momentarily airborne. Because it was packed so tightly, everything fell back into place, even the baby who shrieked with glee, and we careened along the south side of the park to the edge of the sea.

Driving along the eastern coastal road was a visual gift; saltwater ponds, cedar, oak, and pine to the right, and the Atlantic Ocean just a few yards to the left. The small curling waves at the edge of the shore outlined the striated colors of a summer sea.

---

* the "Reliable Self-Service Market" in Oak Bluffs

We rode nearly the full length of State Beach on the Oak Bluffs side, a delicious spiral of expectation rising up in us with the promise of a great day ahead. When we saw the smoke, just a bit before the "big" bridge, El parked the Jeep and got out to let some air out of the tires so we could ride on the beach. While I made sure Baby Linda was still secured somewhere between the snorkels and the corn, El called through the back, "Hey, Susie! Didn't we have the dog with us when we left home?"

I said, "Yeah! Isn't he there?"

She hopped back in, turned the Jeep around, and we headed back to town. We found him a few miles away padding along Beach Road on his way to meet us, still smiling, unperturbed by the tailgate ejection. El made a U-turn and cruised alongside him, matching his pace. He sprang back on to the tailgate as we drove by.

Back at the beach El hopped out, let much of the air out of the tires, slammed the small gearshift into four-wheel drive, and galloped the Jeep over the dunes, Rusty and the tailgate banging away on the bumper.

Before we came to a stop beyond the dunes, parallel to the sea with the tailgate facing the fire, Rusty ran hellbent into the water to rid himself of the newest batch of wood ticks he'd picked up since his last swim the day before.

Smiling and waving, Nelson, his brother-in-law Jimmy Gibson, and my buddy David turned from their work at the fire in preparation for dinner to welcome us. They'd been there since early morning gathering driftwood into a pile, around which they placed a circle of big rocks that they'd hauled from the town dump. A short distance from their fortified fire they had dug a pit about eight feet long, three feet wide and three feet deep. After the men lowered three large wooden barrels into the hole, covered them with a tarpaulin and shoveled sand over the corners, they lay the shovels point-side down along the edges of the tarpaulin and aimed their deep authoritarian voices that meant no nonsense straight at David and me. "You kids stay away from that pit. We don't want anyone to get hurt, y'hear?"

There was no reason we wanted to get near it, anyway, because it was so near the fire and the day was already hot. We cleared out, and the men headed off across the dunes with the baskets and tubes to the other side of the road to go clamming in Sengekontacket Pond.

There they stripped down to their bathing trunks, each a study in red plaid cotton. Tying a length of clothesline to an inflated inner tube that encircled a wire bushel basket and setting a rake and shovel across the top, they pulled their "shellfish cars" along with them as they swam across the channel. Whether they would clam or quahaug* first depended on the timing of low tide. They swam across the channel to the temporarily exposed flats and dug for "steamers" or "piss clams," as we call them, because they squirt a long stream of water if they are out of water and annoyed. Of course, we took great pleasure in annoying them.

Quahaugs lie only a few inches below the sand in deeper

* a thick-shelled clam, pronounced "ko-hog"

water and are gleaned by using (of all the obvious things) a quahaug rake. But Nelson and the guys usually dove down and dug for them with their hands. They placed the clams and quahaugs in the metal bushel baskets suspended in the cool water beneath the inner tubes, to keep them fresh and floating nearby.

While the men worked and played in the pond, David, El and I unloaded the Jeep, stored the coolers under the tailgate to keep them in the shade, and spread the blankets just in time for Rusty to return from his first swim. Racing into the middle of one of the blankets, he grinned at us and shook wildly. By the time he had finished, we'd had our first swim too.

As soon as Rusty found a spot under the Jeep to keep cool, Eleanor dug around in the cooler for some ice cubes to put down between Rusty's paws. I thought she spoke far too sweetly to the critter after he displayed his mischievous sense of humor. Smiling up at her, he licked the ice and sand from his paws and nodded off to sleep.

Everyone got Coppertone application number one.

Wearing only some ridiculous hat and a diaper, Baby Linda held court under the umbrella, punching and kicking the salt air, just plain overjoyed to be outside and near the sea. It was lucky for us and everyone else within earshot that this baby was such a happy little thing. She was content to drink a bottle, spit some Gerber's back at us, and get her Coppertoned face licked by the dog off and on during the day. Her true delight, though, came when El removed her encumbering diaper and sat with her in the water. The rapturous high "E" squeals were the first indication that she was really a mermaid at heart, with a deep and abiding affection for the sea. When she was older and fully under her own power, once she got in the water, there she'd stay until El hauled her out, her chattering teeth and blue lips begging for yet another "last" swim.

Nelson's parents, Nellie and Bill, and his sisters Phyllis, Mary Jane, and Bobby Ann, who was married to Jimmy, arrived, followed by a long winding snake of David's nine boy cousins and little Trisha trailing across the dunes. Only my mother was absent. She's lived on the island since 1946 and has only been to the beach twice. When people asked her why she wouldn't join us, she said, "Ach! How can you stand sitting there baking in the sun vith sand stuck between your toes?" She also cannot swim.

Longtime friends Hilda and Roger Marinho joined us only minutes after they had arrived on-island from New Bedford with a gallon of Coppertone and no umbrella. Roger headed off to help "the guys" and to tell them the latest jokes he'd heard at the pharmacy, jokes that David and I never understood, but jokes that made the adults double over in laughter.

Hilda spread a blanket before she spread Coppertone on every exposed square inch of her already incredibly tanned self. Whether she loved the sunning or talking more, I never knew. She came for two weeks each summer and took advantage of every possible moment of tanning. We kids were delighted because she absolutely adored every one of us, and we her. She could simultaneously hold a conversation with the women about everybody and what they were doing with whom, have a conversation with me about the shells I'd gathered, marvel at the increase in the mass of the boys' biceps (which they measured daily), play with the baby, and never miss a beat of any conversation.

I asked Hilda to swim with me. We walked into the water, a slick of Coppertone spreading from Hilda's legs across the surface. She held my hands while I paddled about in the water at a depth of about three feet and never asked me to summon more courage than the three feet of water demanded. Her patience earned my affection, but I remained scared to death of the ocean. My fear of the sea was unusual.

Perhaps it had to do with a premonition that someday the ocean would have its way with me, a premonition which would be borne out many years later when I got caught in an undertow at South Beach and swept out to sea. After the waves pummeled me on the rocky bottom, the sea spat me out like a watermelon seed with what was left of my bathing suit wrapped around my hips.

Hilda accepted my fear because she shared it. Unfortunately, David did not accept it, but loved taking advantage of it. He did anything he could to get me into the water alone, without Hilda, who allowed no roughhousing in her presence.

We were certainly old enough to swim unchaperoned, so I didn't always have an ally. The boys dragged me off to the water with David shouting all sorts of threats to my life and safety if I didn't play "monkey in the middle," which was actually the only water game I liked. Everything was fine until

David and I had a race to get to the ball. Then, dunking became the agenda, the ball incidental. My scream of "Sto-o-o-o-o-op!" was cut off mid-syllable as David pushed the crown of my head under. I came up choking, ready to bash him, but he was swimming hellbent after the ball as it rode out with the tide. The focus momentarily and blessedly shifted back to the ball, and I was left to crank up my nearly defunct breathing apparatus, amazed by my body's resilience.

Returning with the ball, David and his cousins had a discussion much like the "discussions" I had daily with David. No matter who said what, we played at whatever David decided. In this case, it was playing "chicken."

Bobby Ann and Jimmy's son, John Michael, climbed up Hilda, and Roger's son, Roger Michael, sat on Roger's shoulders and wrapped his ankles around his back. Fighting hand to hand with an identical double-decker mythical beast built of Phyllis's son Maddy and David, they each tried to unseat the other's upper half. Maddy went backwards into the water, and Peter and Paul, Mary Jane's twins, took the upper positions for the next round while Maddy's brothers, Billy and David, waiting for round three. This they considered a big time, especially if the lower halves of the fighting machines were nearly up to their eyeballs in water. They *lived* for this sort of activity, these little Neanderthals, and they called it "play." Not a one of them could fathom how I could resist the delights of near-death underwater combat. They thought I was a sissy. I thought they were altogether unevolved. None of us was wrong. It was not easy for me, Her Royal Highness, the Petite

Poetess of Wing Road, to mingle, "play," and survive my excursions with this battalion of Visigoths disguised as children. But I eventually developed skills to this end, and we all lived to tell of it more or less unscathed, and I even have some fondness for the memory.

When they finally left me to my own devices, I headed straight for my umbrella (not a beach umbrella, but a rain umbrella), my own anti-social umbrella, to read a book. When the women's laughter got too loud for me to concentrate on my story about two little girls enjoying stolen moments on the wharves, I hung the wet towels all around the Jeep windows and made myself a steamy but peaceful little library in which to hide. After a while, even I couldn't stand the humidity level of the Jeep's interior, so I headed off down the beach to collect yet another batch of scallop and toenail shells.

The boys headed down the beach in the opposite direction goggled, snorkeled and flippered, each with a plastic bucket in tow, Phyllis's, Bobby Anne's, and Mary Jane's youngest boys and little Trisha following in a toddlers' mob.

I sauntered down the beach playing a game with myself; picking up only orange toenail shells, but noting where other treasures lay, challenging myself to find them on the way back. I chanted "Maria Teresa Felicia Ferreira Tavares," the melodious fifteen syllable name of Hilda's good friend in New Bedford. I loved the sound of it so much that I would say it over and over to myself when I was alone.

But for our encampment, the beach was deserted. The only sound was the soft lapping of the waves and the diminishing volume of the boys' conversation as I managed to get a half mile away.

Still chanting my Portuguese mantra on my way back, I was picking up a white scallop shell with a calico band when I nearly stumbled into a family that had arrived at the beach. A girl my age introduced herself as Christi, and we started talking very comfortably right away. She introduced me to her mom and dad and younger sister Nancy, red haired and freckled and wanting in on the conversation. But Christi had already claimed me as her friend and suggested Nancy go swimming, so Nancy complained to her mom (typical closely-spaced sibling behavior).

We walked down the beach picking up shells and talking about school and friends and favorite things, discovering that we had lots in common. She said she was from Columbus, Ohio and I thought that must be the very best place in the world because the people from there were so nice. I was delighted to have a girl my own age to talk to, a wonderful reprieve from the competitive nonsense of the boys. She liked walking and reading and sewing and bike riding just like me, and so we were fast friends.

I asked if this was her first trip to the island, to which she responded, "Oh, no! I come every summer for two weeks at the Girl Scout Sailing Camp in Oak Bluffs."

I said, "Are you one of the girls who wears navy blue shorts and bikes by my house every day? I must have seen you a million times!"

I had envied those girls for as long as I could remember,

doing things together and getting to wear those shorts so everyone knew who they were—I couldn't believe she was so lucky. *And* she got to live in Columbus, Ohio!

I liked the fact that I had probably seen her pass by, since the camp and my house were on the same road a couple of miles apart. But I'd never been to the sailing camp on the shore of the Lagoon because I wasn't a Girl Scout, nor did I know how to sail. I thought you had to know that before you went, not that you went there to learn.

When Christi said, "My family comes every year and we stay in the Campgrounds," I began to feel pretty sorry for myself. She got to do all these things, and I only got to live on some old island that no one had ever heard of, except maybe her family. What all the other tourists were doing there escaped me at that moment of despair. "Where does your family go on vacation?" she asked me.

I was embarrassed when I told her I'd never been on a vacation, ever. It was clear to me that my life was a miserable cheat.

We went back to their spot on the beach and made a sand castle with her sister, who was glad for the company. We dug a moat to let the ocean wash in, put some of our shells around the crooked parapets, and stuck sea gull feathers in the top for pennants. When it was finished, we left it for the tide to claim. This was a new concept, playing with kids who were willing to let something go its natural way, astonishingly different from the destructive little soldiers I hung out with.

When the Nowells were getting ready to eat their lunch, I

said goodbye and promised I would walk to the Campgrounds and visit them at the Bishop Haven house where they were staying the following day since they had yet another week on-island. It was the beginning of a friendship that lasted many years.

As I got closer to the clan by the Jeep, I was trying to balance happiness at having a new chum with the realization that I was living an uneventful, luckless, go-nowhere life. Here it was, 1962, I had just turned eleven, and I had never even been on a vacation. My mood was a sorry one by the time I reached our spread of blankets.

I sat down to play with Linda when who should approach but David, the agile marauder, with one blue flipper pointing south, the other north as he refused to take them off to walk on land, slogging his way up the beach, carrying a bucket. His snorkel flailed around on the rubber ring that attached it to the goggles' strap as he arrived blanketside, his eyes staring huge through the dripping goggles.

Because they fit so tightly, the rubber rim elongated the area below his nose, shoving his upper lip down over his teeth, so that instead of speaking, he spluttered. He handed the bucket to El, described the pipe fish, conch, crab and minnows it contained with a wildly flapping mandible and a protruding, immobile upper lip. He finished nearly incoherently with, "Hold thith, don't put it down, the thand'th too hot. I'll get thome more, be right back!" He waddled back to the water looking not unlike a small alien walrus, preparing to yank some more unsuspecting fish from their element.

Lunchtime, which had no specific hour when we were at the beach, arrived. The smell of the linguica grease dripping into the flames snagged our olfactory attention and brought us running.

Each with a paper plate and a bottle of Coke or Orange Crush, icy from the tub, we sat and yakked together, a rare moment of quiet energy. David and I, though, had to have a variation of our daily discussion about whether we would rather have "a million dollars or the moon."

After lunch, we slathered on Coppertone application number two.

We cleaned up and the boys headed for the water, the little ones sporting Orange Crush mustaches and mustard stripes across their cheeks from eating through the middle of their sandwiches. It was Nelson's sister Bobby Ann's birthright to yell a warning (she never missed an opportunity) about full bellies and cramps which was supposed to keep the kids from swimming (but not out of the water) for a short while. I retreated to the "library" to read a story because the baby was asleep, but mostly I thought about Christi and Columbus, letting envy overshadow the fact that I had a delightful new friend.

When the digestive half-hour had passed, the boys came to get me, making my self-pity short-lived. "Come on! Let's go! We're going to the bridge, and *you're* going to jump off!" said the spider to the fly. The long narrow beach that separated Sengekontacket Pond from the Atlantic Ocean had two openings that allowed the tides to flow in and out of the salt water pond. The action of the water kept the shellfish healthy, and the bridges over the openings allowed boat traffic below between pond and sea and vehicle traffic above between Oak Bluffs and Edgartown.

I went to the bridge. But there was no possible way on this earth they could get me to jump off it. I never understood the allure of stepping into an abyss, especially when it'll land you in an outgoing tide. In this case, once you clear the jetty, the very next thing you're likely to see is Spain. For that reason alone, the little ones who were trying it for the first time sometimes stood on the crossbeams, white-knuckled, staring down at the water for three or four days.

They ridiculed and taunted me about being the only kid who didn't jump off. But I didn't care. They told me I was a "yellow-bellied-chicken-hearted-scaredy-cat." They were right. I still didn't care. It simply would not, could not happen.

So they left me sitting on the jetty that ran from the bridge along the cut into the sea. I promised to whoop and clap and cheer every time one of them jumped. I stayed as far away as possible from them for two reasons. One, I never knew when one would sneak over, grab me by the ankles and fling me into the water, and two, I just plain liked to watch. It was a wonderful thing to witness; I experienced its glory as a supportive spectator.

Peter, Paul, Maddy, John Michael, Billy, and little David climbed the bridge, crawled through the slats, and lined up across the very front of the wooden bridge with the outer railing directly behind them, their arms stretched back and wrapped around the uppermost horizontal part of the rail. As they looked out to sea and then down, preparing themselves, I sent them secret encouragement. David and Roger Michael, balancing on the four-foot railing above the younger ones' heads, urged them on.

The little boys stood rigid, like figureheads on the bows of sailing ships, until they leaned into the breeze and fell into the channel. It was the end of slack tide, the period of quiet water between ebb and flow, so they swam easily to the jetty and climbed out grinning from ear to ear.

As soon as the water below was clear of the little ones, David and Roger Michael jumped from the top of the four-foot railing. They arced up into the air, flying, their own propulsion carrying them towards the ozone. Then, for just one fraction of a second, going neither up nor down, they hung there, defying gravity, astronauts. Suddenly the pull of the earth won again and ZOOM!—they plummeted into the sea. Roger Michael did a jackknife. David curled into a cannonball. They swam for the jetty as the little ones lined up on the crossbeams again. They all spread their arms and leapt, landing in six thundering belly flops with a resounding SMACK! on the surface of the water. I winced, imagining what it must feel like to get slammed flat against the stomach by something as large as the sea.

For the boys, who had a liquid recklessness flowing through their veins, the thrill was in jumping off the railing abutting the road in *back* of the walkway. This thrill-seeking group included Roger Michael and David. They left the crossbeams and front railing to the less courageous and instead, from another foot higher and four and a half feet behind the lower railing, they leapt over the walkway that separated the railings as well as over the heads of the little guys waiting to jump. Nearly growing roots into the granite rocks of the jetty, I was riveted with the excitement and fear they neglected to feel for themselves as they flew through the air and cannonballed into the waves.

The water in the channel between the jetties began to move and swirl as the tide came back in. On an outgoing tide, the kids had to swim like crazy to get to the jetty before the rush of water pulled them out to sea. But if it was an incoming tide, other dangers lurked.

The rushing water propelled them towards the barnacle-encrusted stanchions underneath the bridge. Roger Michael and David, old hands at this, breezed between the telephone-pole-sized supports, climbed out on the beach on the pond side of the bridge, crossed the road, and were back in no time.

The next time the younger boys jumped, I saw David's cousin John Michael being pulled through the bridge supports by the tide. He bounced off the stanchion, winced so intensely his features disappeared for a moment, then swam for shore. He hauled himself out of the water, red stripes across his ribs and stomach, trying to hide the pain under the grin-grimace on his face, and ran off, arms flailing, to request first aid from Eleanor. She always had Band-Aids with her for shell cuts and small mishaps. But Band-Aids are useless when it comes to barnacles. El said the same thing she always said.

"Band-Aids are no good for that! What you need is salt water. It's the best healer. Go for a swim!"

And so he was summarily dismissed by the queen of medicine, and did exactly as she said, with much face twisting as the salt water hit the fresh wound. Salt, after all, is used to preserve meat. The wounds eventually stopped running red, and by the end of the day it was just another scar in the making.

Taking a direct hit from a couple of hundred barnacles was not enough of a deterrent to prevent another ten or twenty leaps off the bridge. Soon enough, John was part of the brazen crew again, completing the circuit of leaping, swimming, climbing, and leaping again.

A man who still enjoyed the thrill of unencumbered flight came to jump off the bridge. The boys cleared a path. I thought the splash from an adult-sized beer belly-flop wonderful because it sent hurricane-strength waves whacking at the jetties on both sides of the channel. Eventually, the boys played themselves out, and we headed back to the Jeep.

El and Bobby Ann insisted on Coppertone application number three.

The smaller boys got their greasing first because they were the wiggliest and wanted out of their collective mothers' grasp and into some new mischief as soon as possible. John Michael and the twins came running out of the water with clumps of lapas.* Sporting snorkels and goggles, everyone jumped back into the ocean to gather all they could find. Most everyone loved to eat them.

---

* The Portuguese word (pronounced la-pazh) for a hull-shaped shellfish known in English as a *quarterdeck* or *slipper shell.*

Once we got the shells twisted apart, a thumbnail wedged between the shell and the orange flesh was the best way to detach the small animal from its home. Then with heads tilted back, they dropped the little critters into gullets and swallowed, chewing optional. The process was not unlike what occurs in a fully occupied birds' nest, the gaping mouths of the babies waiting for a tender morsel. Our own baby bird loved them too. Linda got incredibly wound up when the boys lined up like suitors to a princess dangling these raw, slimy animals above her gaping beak. She gulped them down and, unlike the Gerber's pulverized proteins, the lapas never reappeared. She ate ten or twenty before Eleanor interceded the slurpy feeding frenzy, packing the boys off to shuck dozens of ears of corn. Linda, whose full belly pushed against her diaper, took the whole thing in stride, gurgling her appreciation.

When the men returned, one or more of them having gone with Nelson to empty his lobster pots (and possibly to buy more at the fish market if the take wasn't large enough to feed the potential crowd), it was full into the afternoon. They came over the dunes, legal shellfish limits reached, more tanned than when they left to feed the many mouths. They placed all the food in the shade of the Jeep, and put on their deep voices to let us know that it was serious business they were about. We knew what was coming. They felt compelled to say it, anyway.

"OK you kids! Get away from that tarpaulin, now, and stay clear of that fire. We don't want anyone to get burned."

I crawled up in the dunes to watch the theater of preparations. The boys raced to the jetties to haul rockweed off the

submerged stones. They returned, arms bulging with the dripping brown rockweed, tendrils of it hanging around them as
they swarmed up the beach like so many sea monsters. David
was sent back to get buckets of salt water.

Nelson and Jimmy used shovels to roll the huge rocks out
of the low-burning orange embers of the fire. Roger carefully
swept off the sand and pulled back the tarpaulin as the rocks
were rolled towards the rims of the three wooden barrels.
When enough hot rocks had crashed to the bottom of the barrels, the men relieved the boys of their rockweed burdens, and
flung the dripping mass into the barrels, raking the surface as
level as possible. The boys dashed off on seaweed runs again
and again for as long as was necessary. Nelson lowered homemade wire trays covered with whole potatoes and peeled
onions onto the first layer of rockweed. More rockweed covered that just before the corn went in; then rockweed again
and trays of linguica and sausage.

When the foods that needed the longest to cook were
tiered in the bottom of the barrels, Nelson layered the bushel
baskets of quahaugs and clams with seaweed. Nestled in the
top layer of rockweed and crowning this subterranean cornu-
copia were enough lobsters for each person at the party to
have at least one.

Nelson poured a bucket of sea water over each barrel and
the tarpaulin was quickly pulled across the top and secured,
sealing the steaming barrels and their promising cargoes. As
the men began to clean up their paraphernalia, those deep
voices said it one more time.

"You kids stay away from that tarpaulin. It's mighty hot and we don't want anyone to get burned."

It was pretty much understood that now that the men had returned and most everybody's work was finished, the adults wanted to grab a beer and get together for a bit to chat and relax.

So, after Coppertone application number four, we took off.

At this point, El set the watermelon on its side and carved out an oblong piece, then gouged out the pink juicy innards and spooned them onto a tray. Roger started telling the jokes he had saved, and they were all hootin' and hollerin'. Within earshot, David and I just looked at each other and shrugged off a brand of humor meaningless to the uninformed.

Eventually, the platter of watermelon, lonesome for its rind, was ready for us to devour. David and I delivered it to the rest of the kids. In seconds we were up to our armpits in fruit, the juice running down forearms, dripping off elbows, the seeds winging at each other's heads. It was a small but sweet revenge for me when I zinged David with a pit in the middle of the forehead.

While we were in the midst of the watermelon wars, the adults poured bottles of clear liquid into the empty watermelon, along with an occasional can of fruit juice. They refitted the carved-out piece as a cover and poked holes in it, jamming straws through the cap down into the liquid. Once the "juiced" melon was ready, the adults became mobile again. Talking about this and that (which of course, wasn't much in the early 1960s on the Vineyard), they wandered over to the melon where they took pulls on the straws mid-sentence and wandered away again, only to return time after time to the alluring straws.

By now the adults' warnings were more mellow and caring. They said, "Hey, kids, let's not get too near that fire now. You could get hurt."

David and I, being a curious pair (in more ways than one), wandered over to the watermelon ourselves to see if we could pinpoint the allure. Though we were usually discovered and shooed away, that day we actually remained undiscovered up until the time we had our lips wrapped around the straws. That stuff surely did not taste like watermelon. The screwed-up faces we were wearing when they saw us betrayed our actions. It tasted incredibly foul, and made flames stretch from teeth to belly. They didn't even have to say, "You kids stay away from there. We don't want anyone to get burned." It was already too late; we took off for the soda cooler to put out the fire with Orange Crush.

It did prompt an immediate discussion between David and me concerning the adults and their puzzling practices. It was a mystery to us why anyone would willingly return to the watermelon. But return they did, over and over again. If the watermelon "juice" ran out, they filled it up again. Future years would prove that both David and I could solve that particular mystery. But for the time being we were stumped by both the joy of the watermelon and Roger's jokes.

When the tarpaulin had covered the steaming nest for about an hour, we wandered as close as we dared to get a look.

When Nelson and the guys pulled back the tarp, it was as if they had uncovered a volcano. Billowing clouds of steam rushed out of the pit filling the air with the scent of linguica and sea salt. Steam shot into the air and drifted around obscuring the magicians, though hints of what was to come peeped through the thinning vapor. Only when it cleared did we experience the full impact of the magic that had been occurring in the mists below. Dozens of bright red lobsters were nestled in the rockweed. How they went in shaded in dark blues and greens and came out bright red, no one knew. But no matter how many times we experienced this, there was always an audible response of awe from the full company of friends and relatives.

Nelson grabbed the lobsters from the pit and put them on a tray that Eleanor carried to the table. The rockweed was raked out and piled up, the quahaugs and clams lifted out with shovel handles under the handles of the bushel baskets. As the piles of steaming rockweed grew, the men continued to mine this glorious feast.

When everything was on the table, the bright yellow corn and red lobsters, the little round onions and potatoes, and the crescents of linguica teased the taste buds and belly through the nose and eyes.

We all had double paper plates to keep everything steady, and piled as much as we could onto them. Everyone sat down, mostly on the edges of the blankets though some just plunked down in the sand. They spoke a little, moaned in delight inter-mittently, and enjoyed that bountiful feeling that comes from shared work and play.

After dinner the "anticramps" half hour was back in effect. The smell of charred marshmallows filled the air as one or the other of the kids looked away from their toasting at the critical moment. Replacing a fallen marshmallow with a fresh one on a thin driftwood branch, and beginning the process all over again while buddies ate theirs, sweet and golden brown, was a nasty little lesson in patience.

The boys took one last swim and then raced to dry off and get into jeans and sweatshirts to keep off the chill that always follows a full day in the sun. With the evening sky, a languid mood overtook everyone.

Cleaning up was quite a process and was best completed before it got too dark. But there were many hands and flash-lights too when we needed them.

The men raked the steamed rockweed into the holes, and shoveled the sand back in. We kids hauled bucket after bucket of water and poured them on the fire to make sure the embers were really dead. Then we kicked sand over it to be doubly sure. We packed the Jeep, but hardly in the orderly way in which Eleanor had begun the day.

We piled in among inner tubes, bushel baskets and coolers, all coated with salty, sticky sand, as we waved goodbye to each other, disappearing down the paths to the cars. Nelson cradled a sleeping Baby Linda in his arms. We whistled for the dog, who was smiling now because he had lost the ticks and gained the leftover linguica. With Rusty on the tailgate and El at the wheel, we bounded over the dunes towards the road.

As we headed to "the Bluffs" along Beach Road, the sun had set somewhere just beyond Sengekontacket Pond. We were all silent in the Jeep, thinking our own thoughts and relishing the feeling that comes at the end of one of those luscious Vineyard days.

Going through the things that had happened during the day, my thoughts settled on meeting my new friend Christi. I was looking forward to seeing her again, getting to know her better. Clarity descended and washed away my desire to move to Columbus, Ohio so I could travel by car for two days to get to the ocean. Behind my closed eyelids I saw my life in a new way, a miniature watercolor in a pretty frame. I was perfectly happy to be right where I was, on a family vacation on an island, every single day.

When I opened my eyes, we were almost to the little bridge. Long striations of tangerine, turquoise, and indigo reached across the sky in front of us, stretching all the way to Spain.

Taking the Bait

BACK IN THE DAYS when the price of lobsters soared to seventy-five cents a pound, the Martha's Vineyard Bass and Bluefish Derby was held religiously between September 15 and October 15. For those who fished the event, those dates bracketed a sense of excitement that thrummed the very air.

Because most everyone's dad and brother fished the Derby, our tables and freezers reflected the bounty, and frankly, we didn't know how good we had it. Bass or blues for dinner two or three times a week during the Derby was normal in fishing families. Striped bass had once been so abundant in island waters that they had been taken commercially by seine and trap. Who could have guessed that twenty years down the line we would find them so over-fished that a fishing ban would become necessary, and a bass dinner would be nearly unknown in local households?

Oak Bluffs was a Portuguese Catholic community. Fish on Friday was a ritual, a right, and a law for Catholics, Methodists, and Pagans alike, only equal in importance to linguica and baked beans on Saturday night and leftover bean sandwiches on white bread sometime on Sunday.

The tourists were gone, flat-out gone. Island visitors neither lingered through fall nor returned for a now-fashionable "off-season" visit. They left on Labor Day to carry on their own lives, dreaming about but not venturing to the Vineyard again until Memorial Day, because the Vineyard was then singularly a summer resort and held to a rigid schedule of arrivals and departures. Only the few real estate people, caretakers, cleaning ladies and tradesmen heard anything from those migratory thousands by phone or letter between September and May. It was a good system.

Once the Derby kicked in, except for visiting fishermen who were recognizable by their attire of plaid flannel shirts, rubber waders and conspicuous Derby pins, we knew everyone we met on the street. There was a comfort in that, and it added to the rhythm of our lives.

Mornings found fishermen and Derby groupies alike congregated at the daytime center of all things fishy, the coffee shop. Even town politics, grist for the small-town winter mill, had to take a back seat to conversations about what fish were running where, who was "on top," whether or not the position could be held and for how long, success and availability of bait, times of high and low tides, and weather conditions at sea and on shore.

Folks fished all night, when the fish go fishing themselves, returning to town early in the morning for breakfast and exaggerations, the aromas of salt, sweat, and bait competing with the bacon and coffee. Sleep-deprived sons shadowing their dads came in for hot chocolate or coffee (depending on the dad), tired but bursting with the excitement of the rite of autumn on the Vineyard.

Business doors sported the proverbial "Gone Fishing" sign.

"Gone Fishing!"

Anyone who loves fishing knows how little it has to do with catching fish and how much it has to do with soothing the soul. What a premium to also bring home the oceanic bacon! In those days, sport fishing was relatively unknown, certainly unpracticed on the Vineyard. If folks hunted or fished, it was to help support themselves and others. And everyone had their favorite mode of preparation.

Bluefish tastes best in spring and fall when island waters are cold. An oily fish, it is best grilled, baked, broiled or smoked. Old refrigerators, with a hole bored for a smoke stack and a load of slow-burning wood, became back porch smokers to cure the fish.

Striped bass, enormous by comparison, were considered a delicacy, even when abundant. Fillets brushed with a mixture of dark mustard and mayonnaise, garlic, and pepper could be daily fare for fish lovers during the season. No more succulent fish exists than a properly cooked striped bass.

On the last Saturday night of the Derby, my sister, Eleanor, prepared a whole bass that Nelson had caught. As she often did, she filled the cavity with a bread stuffing. The bass was so large she had to rest it on the rack diagonally in order to close the oven door. When this immense fish appeared on the table, its shimmery silver skin had grayed and dried from the oven's work and had curled in little arcs where the scales had been. The stuffing was four inches high, crisp on the outside, awaiting the huge pitcher of steaming Cheddar cheese sauce. As usual, it was magnificent!

After dinner I rode my bike downtown. The door of the Derby weigh-in station always stood wide open. Like the glow of a wood fire, the light spilling into the street and the voices undulating in the autumn air drew me in to this once-a-year milieu. Columns on a huge blackboard leaning against the wall divided information into on- and offshore bass and bluefish categories, weights, and potential island and visitor prize winners. In block letters, Ben Morton wrote current fish weights and leaders' names in chalk, signifying their temporary status.

Friendly wagering and discussion were the real reason the adults were there. I was a silent bystander soaking up the talk and the sense of community, grateful to be involved, however minimally, in the only show in town. I would have loved to have had a more active part of the Derby, captivated as I was by the romance of living by the sea, though I knew no other life with which to compare it. But because it was primarily the domain of boys and men, my nose was not only out of joint, but also pressed against the display window of that particular slice of life. So I visited regularly, vicariously thrilling in the competition, as the leading names changed and heightened my own competitive energy. I celebrated when I saw a woman's name on the boards, sometimes Teresa Baptiste or Betty Bryant. On this particular night, my friend Renee's aunt, Esther Farland, was on the boards with a nine pound, eleven ounce blue. I shouted a silent "Hooray" for Aunt Esther. It was common for women to fish and shellfish with their husbands and families, not so common for them to enter and place in the Derby.

The men enjoyed the competition and some enjoyed even more so the lingering highlight of the story, outlined first with an overview of the weather, catch site, type of bait, time of day, and then with a description of the nibble, the snag, and finally, the drawn-out tale of bringing the fish in. Bass are heavy and take strength and a steady persistence to land. Blues, the toothed hellcats of island waters, require a fisherman with endurance, elasticity of muscle, and enthusiasm for a good fight, qualities not lacking in Oak Bluffs.

So we listened as questions were put to the successful fishermen. They discussed bait: yellow or white pork rinds, blue and silver commercial lures, eels. They answered inquiries about the site of the catch with "Mutton Shoal," "off Wasque," "the Middlegrounds," or "Dogfish Bar." I bit my lips to stifle the giggles, because I knew they were lying through their teeth. Though the uninitiated hung on every word, these fishermen were as apt to give out accurate information as our mothers were when asked where they picked their beachplums for jelly each year. The only thing one could be sure of was that those fish were caught *anywhere* but the site mentioned and the bait was most surely *not* the bait described by the BS artist center stage (BS usually stands for Bait Shop).

For me, the best part was watching Mr. Ted Hartman, the most amiable man in town, a man who, in his gracious old-world way, still tipped his hat to every lady and lady-to-be passing on the street. For every autumn that I can remember, it was Mr. Hartman who manned the scales, calling out the fisherman's name and the fish's weight to Mr. Morton, who wrote them on the boards if the fish was heavy enough to upset the standings.

As I watched that night, men lined up with weighty hopes for the fish they carried. Mr. Hartman tucked his hand under a colossal fan of pink-orange gills, hauled up the fish, and flopped it on the scale. The weight of the falling fish yanked the bucket pan and made the sliders screech, the needle making a rapid tick-a-tick-a-tick-a-tick in its wagging back and forth until quieting for the pronouncement: "Forty-eight pounds, ten ounces." The mounting suspense ended in a predictable "Ahhh!" of delight or chagrin depending who was standing by, onlookers, current record holders, or would-be spoilers.

In the course of a day and night of fishing, hundreds would be caught, though usually only the heaviest weighed in. Extras were always available for the elderly or those who needed a little help stocking the larder. Would that only those in need took the free fish. But this was not Camelot. When someone who could well afford not to dipped into the pile of fresh fish for the taking, not a word was said publicly, but that which is least complimentary flies fastest along the grapevine.

Though I was a part of the Derby in only a small way as an observer, it sweetened my life with excitement at a time when distractions would otherwise have waned with summer's end. It was always after the weigh-in scales and the big blackboard had been stored away for their three-season slumber that the largest bass, the elusive "Monster," would be caught. That fish would taste as fabulous as the rest, would fill a good percentage of the freezer, but would not win the five hundred dollar bond. With the weigh-in station already put to bed for the year, there was nothing left until the following fall but the kitchen table reminiscences and their ever-expanding enhancements.

*   *   *   *   *   *   *

Only when I was much older would I learn the thrill of bluefishing and the soothing journey home across the waves, a sandwich in one hand, a Schlitz in the other.

Home from college, I started fishing with Nelson, setting longlines for cod in the miserable damp cold of April when seaside winter is still something to contend with.

With Nelson at the wheel of the *Escape*, Frank Simmons and I worked together; Frank hauled in line, I coiled it into a bushel basket and hung the clean hooks on the basket rim, our rhythm occasionally interrupted by a codfish flopping onto the deck.

After unhooking and stowing the cod, we hauled in the rest of the line. Then we baited the hooks with raw clams and payed out the seemingly endless line that floated on the surface, suspending the bait below.

It was hard work and cold, that bone-chilling damp seeping through the layers of wool jackets and long underwear. It was more comfortable to let our noses drip than to wipe them with the back of an icy rubber glove. The romance of life by the sea had redefined itself.

As the weather warmed, the number of cod waned and the blues started running. We cruised out to the "middle grounds" in the *Escape* in search of sea gulls, ichthyological honing devices circling and relishing their feeding frenzy, working the fish which were just as likely having dinner themselves. Spotted from afar, the gulls looked like butterflies dancing around the orange weed they fancy, rather than the scavengers they truly are.

Nelson gunned it while we baited the hooks with yellow pork rind. Amidst the working gulls, he dropped the throttle way down, and we let out the lines. The boat rocked lazily along, the lures cajoling and beckoning beneath the surface, a quiet meander jammed with expectancy. Talk was minimal.

And then, WHAM! A rod curled round on itself and Old Frank yelled, "I'm on!" The line payed out with a high-pitched "ZZZZZGGGGGG" ripping the air. To give Frank room to work his fish, we raced to reel in the bait and secure the hooks, leaving the line only slightly slack to reduce the strain on the mechanism. Before we could get to the lines, my rod bent so far over it looked as if it would snap. When I yelled, "I'm on, too!" all hell broke loose, everyone dancing about to clear the deck for the hauling in. A delightful intensity took hold as everyone prepared for action, focusing on one line, then the other.

One feisty bluefish, angry at being duped by a lure, jerked and pulled. This bluefish, like most, would not be large, but it had attitude aplenty and instantly demanded a commitment of time and strength. We fought and wrenched and yanked at each other while I prayed it wouldn't bite the hook and bait right off the line. Fish with teeth! What a concept!

Frank was starring in his own fish battle a few feet away. Predictably, through teeth clenched on a pipe, he said, "Huh-ho! I better bring this fish home to the wife, or I'll have to get a D-vorce," something he'd been saying for fifty years. It made me smile every time.

Since this was my first bluefish, I was hoping I had lucked out and got a slacker. Not so! The powerful push-pull of the fish had me wrenching and reeling in with my all. The sudden slackening of the line sent me ass-over-bandbox across the deck, clenching the rod tighter as I tumbled so as not to lose it overboard. When the fish took off again, I hopped up and braced my thighs against the stern, steadied the rod and hung on for the ride. Yanking and reeling in, yanking and reeling in, Frank and I mirror-danced in syncopated rhythm, and I learned the joy of bluefishing.

I was played out when I had finally reeled all the line in and the fish came "along side," still feisty and capable in its element. The sun reflected off the scales of the fish in a sequin sparkle as it fought the last few moments in the shallows. I was struck by its beauty and was momentarily tempted to let it go. The teasing I would have had to endure would have been life-long. So to keep the lines straight and to stay out of each other's way, I hoisted the shimmery fish up out of the water starboard while Frank worked to port. Once I had the fish on deck I separated the hook from its mouth, its dark blood spilling down my hand.

Exhilaration warred with pity for the fish. I hated seeing those gills gasping for their life-giving liquid air. On the surface the poetic Susie deferred to Susie, the fisherman, but within, personalties had a standoff. Frank tossed his fish in the box. It didn't go unnoticed that I carried the panting fish and set it gently in the fish box with the others. But no one mentioned it, since they each had long ago dealt with the reality that something has to die when we eat.

It was *my* first fish and it was a keeper, so my aching biceps proved. While the others worked at hauling in the fish, I worked at reclaiming the use of my jittery muscles.

The fish box was filling rapidly when a fog bank appeared, consumed the southern horizon, and came roiling at us, all yellow-gray and ominous. At a word from the captain we reeled in the lines, cleaned up bait and rods, and put things away while he headed her home.

A beer in one hand and a sandwich in the other, every one sat back to enjoy the diminishing sun as veils of fog danced between. The spray cooled us as we sat in silence, basking in a feeling of success derived as much from the soothing of the soul as from the catching of fish.

Back at Joe Pina's Pier in Oak Bluffs Harbor, friends and curious strangers waited to see the haul and compare it to the catches of other boats that had already come in. The Escape's catch was put up on the dock blackboard, top slot once again because my brother-in-law, Nelson, the Escape's captain, can smell where fish are schooling.

Everything put away and the boat washed down, Nelson divided the fish among the crew and bystanders and headed home for a bluefish dinner. I went with Frank to the weigh-in station. I hadn't registered for the Derby, so my fish didn't hit the scales. But Frank was grinning about the size of his blue which put him, for a short while, on the boards. The chatter and wagering was lively as Mr. Morton wrote "Frank Simmons, 12.4" in the top slot of "Offshore Blues." Mr. Hartman tipped his hat to me from behind the scales. Nothing had changed; just the way Vineyarders like it.

Second Woods

THOUGH NELSON SAW and heard volumes, he kept his confidences and gave out little information. The occasional gleam in his eye betrayed that he knew things that he would not share. David and I were perpetually on a "need to know" basis, and Nelson thought we didn't need to know much.

So we learned to keep a few things quiet ourselves, like the whereabouts of our camp out in what we called the "Second Woods." It was separated from our houses by a wide field, then the forest that housed my secret grove, and a sand pit, then a huge field again. Beginning around the time we were six or so we trekked out there daily.

Folks here on the Vineyard often disposed of large items by leaving them in the woods as opposed to taking them to the dump. We found things like refrigerators, beds, 2 x 4s, tables, chairs, and all manner of household goods and hauled what prizes we could drag or carry to our protected campsite. Some of the things we found craved fixing, so we slipped into Nelson's cellar, uninvited, and "borrowed" whatever tools we thought we needed.

Now and again Nelson could be heard to say, "You kids

don't know where my crowbar is, do you?" "Crowbar" could easily be substituted with "hammer," "saw," "drill," "cat's-paw," "screwdriver," and myriad other things. We always answered in negative duet, though we both knew full well it was hanging on a nail in a pine tree in the Second Woods or lying rusting in the sand pit. Nelson was on a "need to know" basis.

We never admitted having them. He never accused. But in the end we both knew he knew, and we hotfooted it out to the camp to bring back everything and slipped it all back into his workroom, never realizing it looked any different than when we had absconded with it.

We did ask permission once, though, because we needed *lots* of tools to chop down trees, cut the branches off and secure the new poles together to make walls for the camp we were planning to build. Our hope was to then make a pine branch roof.

When we asked for a couple of saws and hammers, carpenters' aprons, and a bunch of tenpenny nails, Nelson said, "What in God's name are you kids doing out there?" When we told him, he said, "You'd better hope no one finds out about you cutting down those trees. The State Police will fine you twenty-five dollars for every tree you take down, and if you haven't got the money, you'll go to jail."

We were frightened, but of course we did not admit it. On the way out to the Second Woods, Richie Fauteux and his brother, Braddy, helped David and me carry the tools, and we had a discussion about it. We'd already brought down about two dozen trees without telling anyone. We figured those already felled plus the ones we needed would add up to a tidy sum that would keep us all in the clink long past the time we might have planned to have jobs and families of our own. But we took it in stride, knowing no one would be looking way out in the Second Woods anyway.

We got to work as soon as we could, sawing away at those skinny pine trees to make a wonderful forest camp that we hoped would be weatherproof. Of course, just to be sure we wouldn't be discovered without at least a little warning, we decided to post a lookout up in one of the sturdier pines. Richie was the best climber, so up the tree he went.

I had the job of nailing scraps of wood up the side of the tree to make ladder-like steps just like we'd seen in a cowboy movie where the good guys needed to look out for the bad guys. I rolled a tree stump over to stand on and continued making stairs up the tree. When I couldn't reach any higher, I passed up the hammer, extra nails and wood. Richie copied what I did hanging upside down from a limb that could hold him. Then he threw down the hammer and climbed way up in the high limbs to make certain that he could see if anyone came, so we could clear out before we spent the rest of our grammar school years in the brig. The stairway was perfect except for the four-foot gap between where I left off and Richie began the nailing. When he told me he had a good spot and could see all the way to Edgartown, I left him to join the logging crew.

I wasn't strong or adept enough to handle a saw, so my job

was to drag the trees (which we cut randomly to preserve the canopy) to the building site, a task which made me grunt and groan and sweat bullets. Two walls were partially standing from the piecemeal work we had done over the previous weeks. But it surely was not a sturdy structure by any means. We had underestimated the number of pines that would need to be cut. David and Braddy had finished pulling down about six or seven trees and were working on the next one when we heard the deepest man's voice I ever remember hearing, then or since. We froze, the saw stopped in the middle of a tree. The voice said, "Hey, you kids! What're you doing in there? This is the police. We're coming in."

Our little legs turned to stone. But a silent message slipped from one brain to the next. In the same second we all started moving. Everyone picked up a tool and started running. Unfortunately, *my* legs went from stone to rubber, and I could only go three or four steps in any direction before I'd pivot and wind up where I started. I just didn't know which way to run. Then I remembered Richie up in the tree. So I ran all the way back to tell him to come down and run. I called up to him in a loud whisper, not wanting to say his name for fear I'd identify him if the police didn't already know who we were.

He appeared from behind a big branch about as high as a second-story window and I said, "Hurry up and get down here. Why didn't you tell us the police were coming?"

He shrieked, "THE POLICE?"

And down he came, arms and legs wrapped around the tree, his hands trading skin for sap all the way to the ground.

His rear end knocked off and sent flying in all directions every board we had nailed to the trunk, proving that two nails in each step would have been more practical than one. I don't know how he landed alive on both feet. But he did, and we ran as fast as we could to try to catch up with the other kids. Richie was telling me as we ran that he hadn't seen anyone coming, when we spilled out of the dense part of the forest right into a clearing where Braddy and David were standing dumbfounded and speechless. My lungs felt like they were on fire as we looked from them to the "Police."

Eleanor and Nelson were doubled over with laughter, tears running down their cheeks. Nelson had a white handkerchief in his right hand that he had held over his mouth to muffle his voice. The four of us stood there for the longest time just staring at them, our hearts pounding intense rhythms in our chests. The more we stared, the more they laughed. When we finally realized there were no police, we let out a long simultaneous sigh of relief. Nelson, still chuckling, said, "How about you kids call it a day? It's time to go home. But first go get the tools, *all* of them."

The adrenaline kicked in and we all started talking at once, telling our renditions of where each of us had been when we heard "the voice." We went back in, showed El and Nel the camp we were building, and the useless lookout tower. Then they helped us carry all the tools back home.

It took a long time for the adrenaline-spawned jitters to leave, but the rabbit cacciatore dinner that El had cooked helped settle us down, and Richie and Braddy stayed to share it. They went home after dinner, and for the first time in our entwined histories, David and I did not fight over who would wash and who would dry the dishes.

Fearless Freedom of the Night

WHEN WINTER FINALLY released the softening earth from its heartless embrace, our blood careened through our veins, and the itch was upon us. How we loved those spring nights! And how loathe we were to go indoors. In Oak Bluffs, when the winter-spring tease was over, evenings would find us twitching through dinner. As soon as we'd crammed the last mouthful into our faces, we were off, the paper napkins fluttering after us.

We heard it, the soft, humorous whispers of "geetchee, geetchee" coming from the marsh behind Farm Pond. They sang, those pinkletinks,* their tiny one-word song softly at first, as if from far away. It called to us to join the celebration. Once on our bikes, David and I raced down Wing Road and swung behind the baseball park, the frog voices singing louder until we slammed on the brakes and stood in the road that splits the marsh, listening to those millions of wakeful pinkletink sopranos, their whispers now trumpets. The song was made by the expansion of their throats, though we preferred to believe that they made this wonderfully all-consuming noise

---

*local name for tree frogs

which we called "frog music" by rubbing together their itty-bitty knees.

The wetlands surrounding the tiny seaside pond, choked with swamp grass and cattails (which we mistakenly called cat-o-nine-tails), were frequented most visibly by red-winged blackbirds celebrating the advent of spring.

But when spring came, she washed the sea and marsh together through the tiny culvert and gently awakened the pinkletinks one by one to sing the song of the iceman's passing.

Two or three of these Vineyard harbingers were inevitably caught in the flashlight beam of our postmaster, Mr. Hughes, and then in his mayonnaise jar. On the counter at the post office for no more than a few days, peeking through damp greenery, the official mascots of spring would watch us mail packages and buy stamps. A few nights later, Mr. Hughes took them back to the marsh, where they immediately regaled their friends with the tale of their journey, a tale that could be heard all over town.

The din of the festive chorus without and within overpowered all other sound. Our hearts beat to this primal rhythm, part of a cycle we did not yet comprehend. We loved it right up to the point when it became unbearable. When this time came, one of us would simply ride away since no voice could be heard over the frog litany, and the other would know it was time to go to David's for the traditional game of skipsies.

When everybody was assembled, team captains were chosen. David chose Braddy Fauteux, Russell Rogers, Carol Bernard and me. Richie chose Denny Rose, Stevie Steere, and

David Metell. We were all fired up to play skipsies, our rendition of group hide-and-seek. Having freedom to roam the night neighborhood was having the chocolate cake and the lemon meringue pie as well. We ruled, we ventured, we cut a swath of independence through our little town. We were grown, free, fearless, and answered to no one for the duration of the game.

We went over the standard boundaries: south as far as the backyards of Wing Road, east to Dukes County Avenue bordering the Campgrounds, north to School Street, and west to Norris and Pacific, just this side of the cemetery, where none of us would linger no matter how desperate we were for a hiding place.

We dashed through backyards and fields, vaulted over upside-down dories, flew along hedgerows, or scampered across bicycle-cluttered driveways to get far enough away in the dark to tuck ourselves in a bend in the architecture of a neighbor's house, squeezed behind propane tanks, plopped down under old man Gonsalves's grape arbor, squatted between the huge barrels where Joe Bernard boiled the bristles off his slaughtered pigs, sat down in last year's high weeds, all the while trying to control our breathing in case someone from the other team cruised by.

But on this particular night, we decided to change our tactics. Richie and the seekers stayed in David's driveway counting out as loudly as they could. After running for a while, we could tell by the diminishing decibels that we were out of sight.

We ran down Franklin Avenue to the corner of Forest Hill Avenue to have a group meeting by Metell's house. Instead of separating, we planned to rove and hide as a group, then circle back on ourselves from one shadowy concealment to another, staying out of the yellow circles thrown by streetlights. If we got spooked we'd dash under someone's lilac bushes or oil barrel, or melt behind oaks and maples until we determined "the coast was clear."

The flight away and over signified every chase about which we'd ever heard or fantasized. We ran the length of Franklin to Vineyard Avenue with elephant-mounted Huns bearing down on us; fled across the fields behind Vineyard Avenue with hordes of northern marauders breathing down our necks, their banners and pennants ripping in the wind; slogged through the swamp between Franklin and School Streets with an angry posse hot on our trail; raced along Dukes County Avenue with the revolutionary army upon us, their horses's hooves flinging sod, their sabers tearing the sky.

We sneaked through the dirt roads that connected Dukes County, Winthrop, Shawmut and Franklin Avenues and slipped in silence, one after the other, into the dirt. Our whole battalion lay crown to sole in the widest trough of Joe Bernard's freshly plowed field. The scouts from the enemy camp halted not six feet away, arguing about which way to go, unknowingly divulging other hiding places as they tried to guess where we might be. Breath sporadic, eyes wild, we looked for traces of searchlights in the sky. Ears trained on the voices of the enemy to gauge their distance from the foxhole.

We stayed there until winter's dampness, unleashed by the plow, crept through the layers of our torn uniforms, stiffening our flesh.

The enemy had gone back to David's and headed up Wing Road. We rose up, one after the other, like so many wraiths from the grave, and stealthily headed back to Wing Road to line up along the hedges by Bergstrom's house. Our plan discussed during bivouac at Bernard's was to all come in at once and storm the posted guard, thereby saving the gold, toppling the despot king, winning the war. But the enemy camp was hiding behind the very same hedge where we hid. When they yelled en masse, we were shocked out of our skins.

Befuddled and disoriented by the slimy enemy tactics, we broke formation and flew to the four winds. I chose the long run of backyards bordering the woods that separated us from Edgartown miles away. Fleeing the fiends who needed only to touch a piece of my clothing to render me useless to my comrades, I raced through David's backyard, winding up all the setters and hounds that David's father used for hunting birds and rabbits. Sensing I was too large to be rabbit or quail only heightened their interest and they joined the fray, howling the alarm.

Running through the Sylvia's backyard and then through my own, I planned on cutting around the back porch where our houses are close, to fling myself down in front of Ma Phillips's stone porch and roll under the hedges. I looked back, a quick glance, to make sure my assailants weren't too close; an untimely move. In the split second I turned my head, I lost sight of the scene in front of me and ran forty miles an hour straight into the fifty-gallon drum we used to burn our rubbish. It was three quarters filled with wet ashes and immobile. I ran square into it, the impact not unlike that of a parked truck, and fell dead in the field, the air in my lungs knocked halfway to Tony's Market on the eastern front.

The unseeing enemy ran by, not six inches from my corpse, and kept on going. When the stars resumed their rightful positions, I felt a shot of cold air slam into my lungs, and I was on my feet, but not for long. My knees, the first body parts to make contact with the metal drum, had swollen to the size of cantaloupe. I dragged my way to cover in agony.

My mother got out the ice and listened to the story through my tears. When I felt better I tried to persuade her to let me back out to finish the game. She said what she had to say in German, which meant that whatever she was saying could be translated as "no dice." So I was in for the night, wondering how long it would take everyone to figure out I wasn't coming back.

I had some explaining to do the next day because going inside was not allowed during the game. The limp and the bruises helped lend validity to my story, but did not save me from severe teasing about running into the barrel.

While I had been detained in the MASH unit, assigned to a nurse unsympathetic to our cause, I envisioned the others on the run. With naught for company but the stars, the night hid them from the senses of the seekers. Flinging themselves into the swamp, they hid there in the muck, smelly and wet, near dead from exhaustion and loss of blood, but free.

Only when the cold struck marrow did they skulk out of their hiding places, their backs tracing the vertical planes of the neighborhood, and slip, silent as death, towards "HOME," the third post in the fence surrounding David's driveway. With luck the guard was facing elsewhere. Placing the legs just so, they disappeared into the shadow shape of the cedar tree. A clutch of nerves held hearts until the same internal metronome that enables children to fling themselves into a swinging jump rope triggered the signal that caused a silent leap and a dash. Ears pounded with blood as they raced to reach the prize before the enemy, before the shots rang out, before imminent betrayal and death.

Eventually the war-torn squadron disbanded, the warriors headed for their own front doors. Step by step, marching to the rhythm of distant frog music, releasing their fearless hold on the luscious spring night, they transformed back into beings parents would recognize and welcome into the warmth of familiar beds and pajamas sporting baseball players, cowboys, or forget-me-nots.

A Place for Truth

HE SAID THINGS LIKE, "Thou shalt not walk on the grass! Thou shalt not chew gum in public. And thou shalt love poetry." He wore rubber-soled shoes, so we never heard him coming. He sauntered into the room wearing comfortable slacks and a softly draped khaki coat, twirling a pencil. In expansive tones, he said, "Miss Klein, approach the slates and do not disappoint me!"

I went to the front of the room, faced the class, and recited whatever piece of poetry had been assigned for the week, praying the whole while that I had indeed memorized it, and that my oral interpretation would do it justice in the eyes of Harry Dorr.

Harry loved poetry. He worshiped it and knelt passionately at its shrine. Each of the blackboards encircling his junior high English classroom featured a line from literature that Harry admired.

Directly opposite his desk, I sat in the first seat in the first row, not a place of power. I faced the blackboard that had written at the top in pink chalk,

"God is Love."

In yellow chalk, the far right board near the library door, offered,

"To see a world in a grain of sand
And a heaven in a wild flower,
Hold Infinity in the palm of your hand
And Eternity in an hour."

At the back of the room, in white chalk, a line from Shakespeare was written.

"How far that little candle throws its beam,
Like a good deed in a naughty world."

But the one that confused me most, and which I would come to love best, was at the center of the front boards. Taken from Keats' ode, written in blue, it said,

"Beauty is Truth, Truth Beauty."

Because I was a perfectionist and because I didn't know any better, I raised my hand the first day of school while we discussed the selections "on the slates" and boldly said, "Mr. Dorr, the one in the middle is grammatically incorrect."

He swooped across the floor, pointing to what Mr. Keats described as written on a Grecian urn, and in his deepest and most dramatic voice, which was sufficiently deep and dramatic to begin with, said, "Miss Klein, Miss Klein, Miss Klein!" He said it slowly and pointedly. It was the first I'd heard that

"Klein" had three syllables. The reprimand could not be mis-understood.

"Poetry! My dear Miss Klein. The very *best* words in the very *best* order. Grrrrrrrrrrrrammar does *not* apply!" His fin-gers swept the air in increasingly more dramatic curlicues to make his point.

I managed a meek "Sorry" and hid my "Miss-Know-It-All" face behind my book, realizing that I was not dealing with any run-of-the-mill teacher here.

I had come into this class with great trepidation because Harry was renowned for his stringent discipline, his high stan-dards for students' work and behavior, and his no-nonsense attitude. I was deadly afraid of the two years I would have to spend as his student, as was everyone else, because he was now teaching his third generation of Oak Bluffs's children. Trouble with Harry, who was the subject of great reverence in our town, meant worse trouble if word reached home, which it inevitably did, it being a *small* town.

It took but a matter of weeks for my fear to turn to adora-tion as I daily witnessed his brilliance and his teasing sense of humor. He was highly respected because he treated every one of us with respect, always addressing us formally, demanding that we show respect among ourselves.

He was at his very best whenever he found yet another way to challenge any of us, which was regularly. During a spelling test, I asked what the word "placid" meant. Before telling me to look it up (as I fully anticipated), he said, "Let me use it in a sentence for you. Should you live to be one hundred ten, Miss Klein, you shall never be in danger of being labeled placid." Needless to say, I looked it up.

Harry loved words. He read aloud to each of his junior high and high school English classes every day for forty-two years. For that alone he should go down in history as the greatest of men. He was never ordinary, never mundane in his search for the purest form of whatever we were studying, whether literature, poetry or drama.

Every now and then he would simply gaze up at the blackboards, and speak each piece aloud, always believing that people should be surrounded by the beauty of the spoken word. He had a thrilling, passionate voice, as powerful at a whisper as at full volume. And it was always filled with love, for the subject matter as well as, or maybe even more so, for us.

When he finished reciting the selections that embraced us, he would often recite one of the many poems that lived inside him, and then he would finish up with "Beauty is Truth, Truth Beauty." He would say, "Ah, my children, my children! One day you will find your truth and your beauty. Oh, how I wish I could be there to witness those discoveries!" We were too young to understand exactly what he meant. But the measured way he spoke left us all in silence with great anticipation.

I left his class a changed person, fully aware that this was no ordinary human being. He had led me to adore not only poetry of all kinds, but even the works of Shakespeare (at the height of my pubescence, not an easy feat).

In 1969 I finished high school and Harry Dorr completed forty-two magnificently successful years of teaching. His

retirement began, as did my college career. We didn't see each
other for years, except for a rare moment passing in the post
office in Oak Bluffs.

When I had become an elementary school teacher, I
returned to my home town where I was assigned to the last
classroom on the left at the end of the hall, the very one where
I had been a student of Harry Dorr's. When I entered the
room for the first time after all those years, the first thing I did
was to look up at the blackboards. To my great disappointment, the "slates" were gone, replaced by squares of
Sheetrock. It was the early 1970s, and everything in education,
even the very walls, had a somewhat transient quality.

I said to the kids, "On these walls there used to be written
the most wonderful things, poetry of the first order."

When I recited the selections for them, they screwed up
their faces and said, "Huh?" as if I had been addressing them in
a foreign language. Finding them totally uninterested, I went
on to attempt to teach them American democracy, of all the
inappropriate things, and left the vestiges of Harry's legacy
behind. The only thing that remained of those years with
Harry was the scent of old volumes and worn floorboards,
unusual but very real comforts when the day's rewards were
few.

After a number of years I changed careers and found
myself traveling nationwide as a touring storyteller.

I hadn't seen Harry Dorr in my many years. But that did
not prevent me from recognizing his dulcet tones a few years
ago when I was at home for the holidays. The voice on the

phone said, "Good afternoon. May I speak with Miss Klein?"

I said, "This is she."

"What a delight to find you are still grammatically correct, Miss Klein."

I was astonished and my voice betrayed me. "Why, Harry Dorr, is that you?"

"Yes, Miss Klein, I am still alive. I will not long be part of this world, though, and I want you to have one of my volumes by which to remember me. You were always one of the special ones. Please, approach the house and do not disappoint me."

Grinning all over myself, I said, "The truth is, Mr. Dorr, with or without one of your volumes, I could never forget you."

"Come, come, my dear. That's very sweet, but let's be truthful. I'll expect you in fifteen minutes."

Clearly, this man was no fool. Not only did he say I was special, but that he would be departing this world soon. He knew I would come running.

If in doubt, be dramatic.

So I raced to his home, to catch him before he breathed his last histrionic breath. The radio and the television were both blaring as I knocked on the door. I called, "Harry! Harry Dorr!" But there was no answer. I was thinking, Dear God! He wasn't kidding about going soon. And I didn't get here in time, when he swooped out of the bedroom to greet me, and said, "Miss Klein, how good of you to drop by," sporting that incongruous impish grin on that most serious of faces.

We chatted for a while and caught up on twenty years of

experiences. He said that he had been telephoning to offer his former students his books. He named a few, each followed by his or her year of graduation back to 1927. Then he pointed to his bookshelf and asked me to choose a volume. I perused a bit and asked which of the volumes he wished me to have.

"How old are you, Miss Klein?" he said, setting me up.

"Middle to late thirties," I whispered coyly.

"Then 'Miss Middle to Late Thirties,' by this time in your life, surely you must know how to choose, do you not?"

Grinning, I chose. What else? A thick, much-used collection of world poetry.

He took it from me and opening to the frontispiece, inscribed in his boxy beautiful hand, "To Miss Klein, with much affection, Harry Dorr," filling the entire two-page spread.

We sat down at his little kitchen table and talked a bit of this and that and where my former classmates had gotten themselves to in twenty years.

I said, "I wish to thank you for something you taught me a long time ago that has stood me well all these years. You were always so very different than anyone else in town. As a matter of fact, you modeled being different every day that I spent with you. You carried yourself with such grace, because you knew who you were. I thank you for that, for teaching me that it was all right to be different."

"Different?" he said with great undulation in his tone, "Different? Dear God, Miss Klein, at the very *least*, be different! And I don't mean perhaps!"

I should have seen that coming. "Well," I said matter-of-factly, "it's as good as done!"

He'd lost not a wit of his exuberance for life. I said, "Do you remember what it used to say on the blackboards around the room?"

"Of course, my dear, how could I forget? They were there on the slates for forty-two years.

'God is Love.'

You do recall, Miss Klein, that comes from the Bible?" I nodded unnecessarily.

" *'How far that little candle throws its beam,*
Like a good deed in a naughty world.'

"Ah, Shakespeare said it so beautifully.

'To see a world in a grain of sand
And a heaven in a wild flower,
Hold Infinity in the palm of your hand
And Eternity in an hour.'

"Blake was indeed a master! And your favorite, Miss Klein?" he said, raising one eyebrow,

'Beauty is Truth, Truth Beauty.' "

Time had stopped. I was simultaneously buoyed up and cradled by the passion in his voice. It was wonderful to hear him say those words again. We just sat together in silence for a while, the memories drifting round. I left a small present, wished him a Merry Christmas, and said goodbye.

Instead of driving me home, the car somehow went straight to the school. When I arrived there, I went to the principal's office and asked if I could visit the room at the end of the hall. He said, "Sure! The kids will love to see you. They'll expect you've come to tell stories."

I said, "I'm off duty today. But I want to check something."

Upon entering the room, by now midafternoon, I saw that the winter light was slanting through the west windows bathing the room in yellow light the way it always had.

The kids asked for stories, but I declined.

"A long time ago when I was a student in this room, we had blackboards," I said, rather far off in my thoughts.

The kids, nearly in unison, said, "There are blackboards now. What are you talking about?"

When I actually *looked* I saw that the slates really *were* there. They had not been removed, as I had thought, just covered up. Now that the Sheetrock and the 1970s were gone, they were once again unveiled.

Because the afternoon rays filtered through the room at a slant that is only found on the New England coast in winter, a glint of something shimmery at the top of the center slate caught my eye. I stood on my toes to get close enough to the blackboard to see what I knew had to be there.

Though the words had long since been erased, those poetic selections had been written and rewritten so frequently over Mr. Dorr's long career that there had been some action of chalk and slate. The colored chalk is gone but the shadow of the words remain.

So now, on a small island off the Atlantic coast in a second-story classroom, the light of an early winter afternoon slanting at a particular angle through the west windows illuminates some very old slates. Because a man dedicated forty-two years of his life to the expansion of the minds of his students, lovingly exposing them to poetic words of wonder, one can see that it says,

"God is Love."

On the slate at the back it still says,

"How far that little candle throws its beam,
Like a good deed in a naughty world."

Near the old library door, it says,

"To see a world in a grain of sand
And a heaven in a wild flower,
Hold Infinity in the palm of your hand
And Eternity in an hour."

Best of all, though the blue dust is gone, it still says,

"Beauty is Truth, Truth Beauty,"

and it's etched in stone.

Fishing the Rip

ONE BLISSFUL AFTERNOON when El, Nel, and I were fishing the rip* off the Chop† aboard the Escape, I hooked a bluefish. As usual, a battle with the fish ensued. It was flapping so hard when I got it into the boat that the fish swung in an arc across the deck.

Nelson left the wheel to help me. He snagged the fish out of the air and was taking the hook out of its mouth when the boat hit the rip. Caught in the currents, the boat rocked like crazy, and one point of the three-pronged hook plunged into the soft palm flesh between Nelson's thumb and forefinger. Eleanor, coming up from below to see why we were being tossed about, saw no one at the wheel. Nelson called to her to get the cutting pliers. With a leap, she had one hand on the helm, pulling us out of the rip to avoid capsizing, and the other fumbling in the toolbox.

The fish was still very much alive and now joined to Nelson. Displaying no emotion, he told me, "Grab the fish and hold it tight," as the struggling fish yanked the hook further into his hand.

---

* an actually visible undulating line of calm running along the edge of rough sea where opposing currents meet, generally situated off a point of land
† a local term meaning headland, as in East Chop or West Chop Light-house

Blood and guts have never been my forte; dealing with them always causes gravity to catch at the back of my knees. I considered jumping overboard. But rather than be named a sissy, I acted totally against my own nature. I grabbed the poor fish so tightly that I squeezed the life out of it as well as its entrails, which squirted out the bottom onto my boots, while its eyes nearly exploded out of its head.

When El had righted the boat, I was still struggling to stay conscious and hold the fish as steadily as I could so she could cut the prong in Nelson's hand free from the rest of the hook and the fish.

With not just a little growling and grinding of teeth, El cut through the steel. Nelson, on the other hand, said nothing, but had his face set in the scowl I recognized as annoyance. He pushed the point of the hook through his hand and out the other side. Blood drained from his hand onto the deck almost as quickly as it drained from my face.

Nelson got out his handkerchief and wrapped it around his hand, and I sat down with my head hanging between my knees, battling unconsciousness, still choking the life out of a dead fish. Eleanor, back at the wheel, opened up the throttle to get us back to the harbor to head for the hospital. When they pried that fish out of my paws, I was still somewhere between consciousness and "un," looking at the world from the viewpoint of the fish.

For me, killing something barehanded was brand new, and though I had done it under duress, it left me weak-kneed and pensive.

A Scent of Oils

THE BASEMENT APARTMENT walls were brown, as were the furniture, the bedding, and the dress Kate was wearing. Already in that span of delirium between worlds, recognizing loved ones was beyond her. She lay on her bed fidgeting with the bed clothes, her eyes closed, her skin a yellow gray, like old laundry. When my mother answered my question concerning the congested sound accompanying Kate's breathing and called it "the death rattle," I sat down next to Kate. Though her flesh looked brittle as onion skin, to the touch it was silky. With one finger, I stroked the protruding veins of her hand to the rhythm of the rattle, while I fought to strike a balance between revulsion and duty.

The recoiling thirteen-year-old in me wanted to flee. But another part of me resonated with a distant memory of what I had once known, and I did what I must have done a thousand times before. I sat with her and witnessed the "becoming," the metamorphosis of an energy form, shedding one stage for another. She was ready. Only a tenacious heart muscle prevented her from a swift release through the veil, as the rattle measured out her remaining moments, chipping at time.

The dinginess of the apartment revealed that Kate had

lived entombed for some time, and I thought her transition to light might be a shock. Mrs. Spencer saw me taking in the surroundings, and she saw the impact on me. She took my hand and said, "I believe you desire the light. Come with me."

We road in an elevator with a folding latticework door upstairs to her apartment. I was startled by the contrast of her well-appointed penthouse, its air and light dizzying, as if I had been breathing darkness as long as Kate had. With a delicate gesture, Mrs. Spencer ushered me to a black lacquered chair. I sat on the cushion of rose moire satin as gingerly as I could because I felt I was intruding on a museum exhibition. I spoke only when spoken to and hoped to God I'd remember my manners, trying the whole while not to stare at her.

I had had a curiosity about this woman since I first heard the urgency of her voice on the phone a few days before. Having never met her, I thought it eerie that I recognized her voice as one does the tinkling of a familiar bell. She had said that Kate often spoke of my mother with great fondness and so asked my mother to come because Kate was seriously ill. In the dark fog of Kate's cavern, I could only discern that Mrs. Spencer was tall. Here in the light she was visually arresting! Her well-tailored navy silk dress and full Gibson hair style, which added to her height, were anachronistic contrasts to the love beads and granny glasses we had seen earlier at Penn Station. If her dress was uncommon, her face was remarkable. Thin painted eyebrows (that expressed far more than her well-chosen words) arched over eyes that were at once kind and knowing. What should have been an obvious resemblance

to Aunt Fanny's eyes escaped me. Her remaining features,
lightly powdered and rouged, presented only the subtlest
topography. I'd never seen such a face, so strange and riveting.

With the late winter light playing watery shadow games
on the pale walls, I could not help but compare it to the apartment four stories below. I was perplexed by Kate's choice. She
lived in a darkness so dense, I could sense the molecules slip-
ping by me when I walked through her rooms. Even a little
paint would have made a huge difference. After much thought,
I decided it could only be a matter of money. She couldn't
afford the light, I thought. I was wrong. On her death we discovered that though Kate appeared poverty stricken, she was
not. What I thought at my tender age to be a substantial
endowment she left to a well-known children's home. It was a
detail of the life of this tiny old woman that further confused
me. I was privy to these details only because Mrs. Spencer had
been executrix of Kate's will and had told my mother, who in
turn told me.

It came as a great surprise to my mother to find she had
also been named in the will. Kate had told Mrs. Spencer that
the gift was in return for a chicken dinner my mother had
shared with Kate and her husband in 1941 during the
Depression when they had had nothing to eat. The modest
bequest purchased an airline ticket that allowed my mother to
return to Germany, a hope she had cherished for thirty-seven
years.

For me, the gift from Kate was the chance to begin a
friendship with Mrs. Spencer, who lived on New York City's

chic Park Avenue in winter and, astonishingly, in the Oak Bluffs Campgrounds in summer. She lived not just "*in* the Campgrounds," but in the very cottage which personified the Campgrounds, the Pink House, the only house (at the time) that was worthy of being depicted on a postcard.

After her arrival on the Fourth, I went to see her for the first time. There was a music about the place, a soft purring of the leaves in the ever-present breeze. A Victorian house is a beguiling sight in and of itself. But one painted rose, burgundy and white, and set against the dark green of oaks, is truly a vision straight from a fairy tale. Because of the tasteful shades Mrs. Spencer had chosen, it had a charming elegance unknown since her tenure there. The porch boards creaked, of course. I ran my fingers along a curved line of lathe work on the porch railing. Thin packaging cord was strung across the palest of pink antique wicker chairs on the porch, a sign to stranger and tourist to gaze and appreciate, but to stop short of intruding. Having only encountered the outside of the house, I was thrilled to be beyond the chair cords, poised to enter. A knock on the wooden screen door brought the overlapping resonance of the rap as well as the clatter of the ill-fitting door against its frame, testimony to the moist salt air.

Through the screen my eyes took in the room with the steady pan of a cinematographer's camera: white vertical wall boards, gray wide board floor, white wicker, antique and ornate. The uninsulated interior walls which were also the exterior walls were lined with the supports that held the house together. The contrast of still life florals and the woven black rugs with pink and green blossoms made the room a sweet dream. A scent of oils swept the room on the sea breeze drifting from back door to front, clinching the memory. My camera eye rested on her easel bearing a nearly completed painting, which slanted towards the huge paned studio windows, catching the light. Bright mounds of color shone on a working palette set down for a moment on the small table next to her subject, red and white carnations in a wine red vase.

For a moment, I almost didn't want her to appear. The room mirrored her so well, I thought her actual presence might be redundant. When she came from the kitchen at the back of the long room, her graceful stride stirred the air only slightly, the dust doing a lazy dance through the sunbeams. She removed the tiny hook that held the screen. Her table was placed in the small alcove between the easel and the kitchen, facing a set of gothic doors with etched frosted glass windows that were always open to the breeze. We ate what was to become our standard fare: chicken salad sandwiches on Pepperidge Farm white bread and iced tea with a sprig of fresh mint. I helped her do the dishes in the old sharp-cornered metal sink that still had a pump, and we filled in the gap since our last visit in March with chatter. Our lunches became the first of two rituals. The second began with my next visit.

Because her love of flowers was evidenced by the floral still lifes throughout the house, I crawled around the old abandoned stone foundation across the street from my house, picking pink and white sweet peas and wild yellow roses. Soon after I arrived, the bouquet graced her lunch table.

When we were through talking, she let me watch her paint provided I was quiet, an easy task since I found her efforts at the easel mesmerizing. She chose her colors from a heap of crumpled metal tubes, squeezing worms of cerise, cadmium yellow, cobalt, and little mountains of white onto her palette. Watching her mix them together gave me goose bumps. She and the brushes swirled and layered the unsuspecting colors until they lost their identities and became, instead, a known thing. All the while, her elegant strokes were a dance of wrist and hand.

But the first time I saw her slap a glob of barely mixed red and white onto the canvas with a tiny cake server, smearing it all, tumble down, back and forth, I thought her mad. No sane woman would deliberately hurl paint onto a canvas.

The unexpectedness and aggressiveness of the action took me by such surprise; she surely would have heard my intake of breath had she not been on a flight of her own in conspiracy with the colors. As she smeared the paint across the canvas, some completely foreign sensation gripped my lower spine, which seemed infused with the new pigments. I felt them backing up and rushing about in my veins and thought they would surely spill out my fingertips. The colors had somehow gotten inside, making me flush and sweat, and still she slathered around in the paint.

The journey of those ruthless colors rendered me uncomfortable and yet filled me with an uncommon joy. It is my first recollection of the pain-pleasure that accompanies the creative impulse. I was in a slight panic when I finally saw the intended inflorescence, and I thought I could calm myself. But with that vision, the roof blew off the house of what I knew to be true. The walls fell away, leaving me standing exposed to a hot wind. I had caught glimpses of this elusive thing in my dream states, warning and then assuring me that there really were other ways of sensing.

As she wiped the paint off the palette knife and set it aside, I saw its path had left not only exquisite racemes of pink sweet peas on the canvas, but also a glorious experience for me to savor for the rest of my life, that of the transient yet sublime thrill of the creative impulse's samba with the soul. The sultry colors, having traversed my entire circulatory network, returned to the palette, leaving me imprinted and forever changed. I said nothing. But when I left her house that day, I felt I had become a two-dimensional animated outline of myself teetering along a path that only hours before had been familiar.

I was welcome to visit as often as I pleased, and it pleased me to visit often over the next three summers. I went whenever an hour presented itself, a sweet respite from the turmoil of adolescence and my restaurant dishwashing job.

One day Mrs. Spencer asked if I'd be interested in seeing some of her other work that was hanging elsewhere but had been photographed. By that time I was sixteen and delighted to have a chance to see another facet of her work.

I sat on the settee and flapped open a huge album to find bouquet after bouquet and then portrait after portrait of stern judges in robes and society women in pearls and satin. Then, of all the surprises, there was a photograph of a portrait she had done of Eartha Kitt posing in the wings of a New York theater, as well as Rex Harrison and Julie Andrews in their costumes as Henry Higgins and Eliza Doolittle when they starred on Broadway in "My Fair Lady." I had memorized the score from the record my mother had brought back from New York City, and frankly I thought that Julie had better move over, because I was certain I was Eliza's incarnation. The thought that she had not only met them but enjoyed the intimacy that must develop between artist and subject occupied me for days.

She executed the portraits much differently than the florals. I could see that, even with my limited knowledge of painting. The portraits, though painted flat on the canvas, gave me a sense that the person depicted might speak aloud. When I told her so, she asked me to sit for her. Delighted to be asked, I found it easy to sit for long periods, staring off into space. It was something I had mastered ages ago. Off dreaming in one of my fantasies, the only sense I had of being in that room was the scent of oils and the occasional tingling I would get on face or scalp that suggested the feature of her concentration. The days slipped away, measured by the petals of the yellow roses dropping silently to the table around the blue vase.

In the middle of a session one day, she announced it was finished and said, "Come, take a look. Tell me what you think." I stared at it a long time. The face was of someone older, someone sparked by a fire that shone right out of her eyes, as if in the trance that overtakes when speaking from distant memory. I found it alarming and wasn't sure I liked what she had done. I couldn't say what I thought and remain polite. So I said nothing. Mrs. Spencer pressed me to tell her what I thought of it, "honestly," she said.

I took the deep breath that precedes telling a reluctant truth and said, with some disappointment, "Well, it looks like a member of the family that perhaps I haven't met yet. But I'm not sure that it's me." I was surprised to see that that made her smile pleasantly.

With an expression most serene, she said, "Ah, Susan, it is you, most assuredly. But it is not you now. It is whom you will become." And with that pronouncement, I had to be satisfied.

We went back to our visits that each began with the presentation of a bouquet of roses and sweet peas as long as they continued to bloom. Linda, who was no longer a baby, was frequently in my charge in the summer. Mrs. Spencer thought her a wonderful child and encouraged me to bring her with me. I did, but kept the visits brief, since the little one was hard to contain, and always wanted to be at the beach. When she asked me if I thought it would be all right to bring Linda to sit, I said I'd ask her parents. El and Nel agreed it would be a wonderful opportunity to have the portrait done. Wiggly Linda had other ideas. But we struggled through. Mrs. Spencer loved Linda's hair which was long and had many shades of blond. Braided, it showed off the variations of color in a beautiful undulation secured by blue ribbons at the ends. The six-year-old sprite struggled to keep still, only appeased by promises of long afternoons at the beach following the modeling sessions. But when it was finished, it was *she!* In her mysterious way, Mrs. Spencer had caught that look of mischief in Linda's brown eyes, and the seriousness of her mouth captured both a sensuality and petulance. A photograph of the portrait was made so that Eleanor and Nelson would have a rendition of it until it could be purchased.

I continued to visit Mrs. Spencer as often as I could. But it was the last time that I enjoyed that luxury, because I worked full-time the following five summers at the theater after my graduation from high school. Full-time in a struggling theater means the actors are also the set constructors, costume designers and seamstresses, box office personnel, and the gophers who hang posters, type scripts and clean up the theater. I never had spare time and rarely saw Mrs. Spencer thereafter. Once college finished, I had only an occasional correspondence with her.

When I had my first teaching job, my kindergarten and first grade students were doing life-size portraits of themselves. I thought having a real portrait of someone they knew might be a good inspiration. So I wrote to Mrs. Spencer and asked her where the portrait of me was, and if I might be able to borrow it.

I was completely surprised by her answer. She wrote that the portrait of me no longer existed, that it had been painted over.

"How will I know if it's whom I've become?"

I said it out loud to myself in disbelief. I considered it a huge loss and didn't really know what to do with the ache I was feeling over the disappearance of my "face," nor the blow to

my ego caused by the awareness that my portrait wasn't important enough to her to keep. But as with all things, time healed,
and I let go of the wound, accepting her decision as one of
those changes over which I do not have control.

The years drifted by, and our relationship was relegated to
Christmas card exchange. My Christmas cards were conven-
tional. Hers were always photographic renditions of her
paintings on the palest pink paper, the exact shade of her
wicker porch chairs. Eventually her health became precarious,
the beautiful pink house was sold, and finally she stopped
coming to the island in summer.

A number of years ago, a phone call from Ruth Anderson,
a longtime friend of Mrs. Spencer, brought news that her will
bequeathed her entire collection of paintings to the
Andersons, Ruth and her husband, Carl. Mrs. Anderson
wanted to verify that I was the girl in one of the portraits in the
collection. I assured her that the painting of me no longer
existed in its original form, or so I had been told by Mrs.
Spencer. Mrs. Anderson said that it did indeed exist, was one
of Mrs. Spencer's favorites, and hung over her desk until she
died.

A few months later, the Andersons had it removed from
storage and shipped to the From The Heart gallery on the
harbor front, as the owners, Joyce and Judy, were considering a
show of selections from Mrs. Spencer's works. Just as I had
made arrangements with Judy to see the portrait on my return
from a three-week performance tour, I received word from
Mrs. Anderson.

"The painting is waiting for you," she said. "But we discovered a name in Jean's handwriting on the back of the portrait which says 'Linda,' though Mrs. Spencer always maintained it was you."

I asked only one question. "Braids?"

"Yes," she said.

"It is Linda, then. She's my niece."

It was with mixed feelings then that I went to the gallery. All those years of having looked forward to seeing my portrait to discover if it was whom I had "become" had filled me with anticipation. Knowing that my portrait was lost forever was disappointing. But I knew the other portrait would have its own allure. What I didn't count on was being completely overwhelmed by the sight of Linda's sprightly little face.

When Judy handed it to me, reality fell away, and I stepped into the painting. I was surrounded once again by white wicker, filtered sunshine, and the scent of oils. Mrs. Spencer was there fleetingly with that sly smile, all grace and knowingness, holding me in a gaze that spoke of her ability to "see." For just that momentary crack in time, she stood there looking at me, filling me with those important small truths she had taught and I had forgotten.

Then I looked at Linda. It was an exquisite rendition of the child, a bracing reminder of all that I had forgotten. Her eyes, so much like her father's, evinced a depth of emotion that could not be spoken, but shouted to the sky nonetheless, without benefit of words. I stared at the part in her hair, tanned by the summer sun. She reached up to hold my hand as we walked the path to Mrs. Spencer's pink house, lost in our chatter. It took a minute or more to "land" and recall that I was gazing at a portrait and not another time and place, and that Linda now has children of her own.

I left the painting at the gallery and went immediately to my mother's house. I told her I had seen it, and we made the only decision possible. With splendid generosity, the Andersons parted with the first piece from the collection to ever be sold. When Jettche and I went to their house to retrieve it, we spoke about the collection of paintings and the last years that they had enjoyed with Mrs. Spencer's company. Mr. Anderson spoke a language I understood when he said, "The viewing of Jean's paintings has the same effect on me as the scent of good perfume."

*   *   *   *   *   *   *

On Christmas morning the portrait was wrapped and rewrapped, disguised in an appliance box so no hint would be available to my sister, Eleanor, or Linda, Christmas present detectives sly enough to give Sherlock a run for his money. My mother, Linda's younger sister Tracey, and I had kept it a secret. As Eleanor and Nelson together tore at the huge quantity of wrappings and packing materials, we all watched, some with curiosity, my mother with an anticipation that wound her so tightly she was nearly pinging.

When the last layers of tissue paper fell away, the appearance of that face sent ripples through all of us, tears springing everywhere. Even sleepy Baby Nelson, only eleven days old and cradled in Linda's arms, must have felt the aftershock of a piece of the family puzzle falling into place. Something in that moment shifted. In a single reflex action, the portrait was up on the wall and we took it in. As I told of the discovery of the portrait, the phone calls, time lapses, confusions and mistaken identity, and of bringing the painting home, we all shared something we did not speak. Something had been misplaced, thought lost perhaps. The story of its journey home brought to us what the ancients had always known was the single most important gift: the family story, that pulse that twists and turns along the vine of common identity, the priceless reminder of who we are.

The following morning when the house was relatively quiet, I came around the corner from the kitchen into the living room to find Linda's seven-year-old daughter, Amanda, staring up at her mother's portrait. In her red and white nightgown, her braids loosened from her night's sleep, she stood transfixed. Taking my hand, she said, just above a whisper, "Susie! It looks just like me! "

I had wanted the words of the artist to be true, had wanted the experience of the portrait coming round on itself. And so it had. Mrs. Spencer had said, "It is who you will become." And she was right. The scent of oils bequeathed a "becoming" after all; its affirmation lives in Amanda's face and in my telling of the tale.

Ruby Window II

A FEW YEARS AGO, when my mother and I found ourselves once again by the sea picking beachplums, I wandered off across the dunes where I discovered low-bush plums in grand abundance. Knowing it would make for easy gathering, I settled in for a delightful afternoon.

Jettche was closer to the car, talking a blue streak to the plums about their good fortune. I figured she'd be fine there, even though it'd been a hellish year with too many trips to the hospital, a plethora of prescriptions, and a diagnosis of congestive heart disease. When I suggested that she stay home and let me deliver the beachplums to her, she said, "Vhat, are you crazy? They said I vas sick, not DEAD!"

So there we were. I was picking gobs of beachplums with both hands, one pot already full, the other filling rapidly. When I heard my mother calling my name at the top of her lungs, the fear in her voice sliced through me, and I jumped to my feet, sending fat plums rolling in sixty directions. I started running in the direction where I had left her, but once I reached the highest point, she was nowhere to be seen.

She kept screaming, "Susanna! Help me!" and I kept

screaming, "MA!"

In those early minutes when an emergency presents itself, it's amazing how many images of possible disaster pass across the mind's eye. One part of the brain ticks off the scenes that might be occurring. The other part of the brain rolls through the options of how to react and where to find help for each concocted possibility, all in the small space of a few seconds.

As I slipped and tripped over the sand, my adrenaline roared through me, pounding in my ears. Where is the nearest phone? The nearest house? How long will the ambulance take to arrive? Where will I find someone to come and stay calm and let me scream?

"Susanna! Help me!"

"MAAAAAAAAAAAAAAAAAAAAAAAAAAAAAA!"

Every cell was screaming, "I'm coming, Ma," as my eyes swept the landscape trying to find her, and my brain considered a half-dozen horrific scenarios at once.

And then I saw the shoes.

Sensible shoes.

Sticking straight up they were, heels to heaven, waving just over the top of a three-foot beachplum bush. When I reached the bush, I tried to keep my voice from betraying my complete and total fear that these were the last moments we would have together before her death, which I was going to have to helplessly witness.

"Ma! What happened? Are you hurt?" gushed out of me. And then I saw fully what had happened. There she was, eyeglasses askew, housedress wrapped up around her torso exposing her white slip, her ever-present apron poised in the air where it was pierced by the plum bushes, and her pantihose striping up and down her legs. She was completely upside down, clutching her aluminum pot.

"Ach, du lieber, Susanna, can you see, did I drop any?"

"Did you what?" I said, out of breath.

"Did I drop any beachplums?"

Slowly, a small piece of me swam through the flood of adrenaline to get a grip on the ridiculous reality of the situation; only a small piece, though. The rest of me was still in "Hyperspace 911." I heard my own voice say, "No, Ma, it's okay. You dropped not a one."

Calm was the voice, though the rest of me was flailing; arms up and down, hands through the hair, one foot in the sand, the rest of me pivoting round it, the adrenaline like a fog too thick to think through.

Emergency! I thought. Wasn't there an emergency? Isn't she dying? Isn't death leaning on a fence post nearby, picking his teeth in anticipation of this lively morsel?

No. No emergency. She's alright. She just took a header into the bushes and somehow landed face up. No. No emergency.

And then, finally, clarity. WHAT? NO EMERGENCY? Oh, yes there is! There's an emergency all right. I'm gonna kill her!

As all that "drama juice" searched for a place to go, I heard my mother say, "Vell, don't just stand there! Help me! I'm schtuck!"

It took me a while to extricate the old girl from the bushes that gripped her. Even with all the yanking and pulling, she was only a little worse for the wear. But those panty hose, they were a wreck!

When she was right side up again, I managed to calm down and return to my spot where I recaptured half a pot of fallen plums. We got quite a harvest that day. The trip home was filled with retellings of each side of the story and not a little teasing.

When we arrived at her house on Wing Road, she covered the beachplums over with water. The annual process had begun. As usual, it went through cleaning, boiling, straining, sweetening, boiling again, skimming and testing. When the jars were filled and the panela was in the sink, the kitchen curtains and my mother smelled like that luscious substance. There was a saucer of cooled froth waiting for me on the table, its color … beachplum pink. As I smeared it across a piece of sweet-buttered rye, she held the first jar up to the sunlight streaming through the window and said, as I imagine she will say every year, "Look at that, mein Susie. Can you see that little ruby vindow right there in the middle? Ach! Vhat a vonderful thing, a beachplum!"

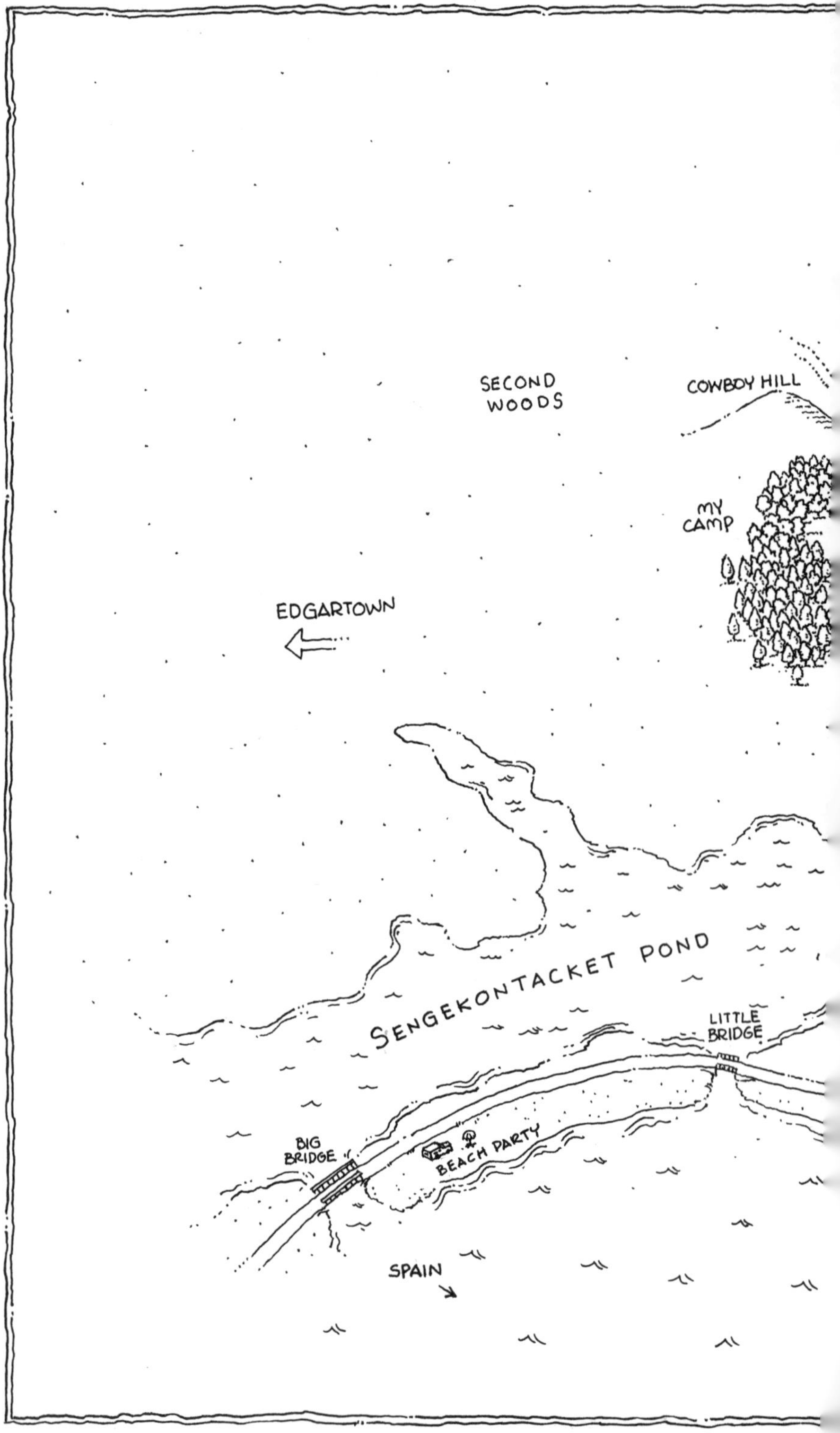
SECOND WOODS
COWBOY HILL
MY CAMP
EDGARTOWN
SENGEKONTACKET POND
LITTLE BRIDGE
BIG BRIDGE
BEACH PARTY
SPAIN